DARYL LOVE

Ride or Die 2

The Queen's Move

First published by Rich Dog Entertainment 2025

First edition

Cover art by Chemieka Amuzu

This book was professionally typeset on Reedsy.
Find out more at reedsy.com

I thank God for the vision, imagination, and journey that helped shaped my stories and strengthened my voice. To my family, friends, and everyone I met along the way who inspired and supported me, thank you. To my illustrator, thank you for bringing my vision to life and helping me build a legacy worth remembering. And lastly, I thank myself for enduring every chapter and continuing forward with faith.

Contents

1

Dreams of Freedom

"As for the charge of conspiracy to the possession of a controlled substance with the intent to sell, the court finds you GUILTY!"
GUUUUILTYYYY!
GUUUUUIIILLLLLLTYYYYYYY!
Eight years!
Eight yeeearrrssss!
EEEEEEIGHT YYYEEEEEARSSSS!
   The judge banged his gavel in slow motion, and with a devilish grin on his face he repeated: "GUILTY."
"GUUUILTY."
"GUUUUILTTYYYYYYY."

* * *

"Inmate 12677… LOVELESS!" Sgt. Reynolds yelled out from the officer's station.
   Cookie woke up from her sleep, hearing someone calling her. She had been having the same dream over and over for months now, playing back her day in court. Years had passed and it still seemed unreal to her, but she learned to adapt.

1

She glanced around the dorm to see who called her. All the other girls were still asleep, then she noticed Sgt. Reynolds waving for her to come to the officer's station.

What! she thought with a sigh, as she slipped on her slippers and headed up front. She groaned with every step as she tried not to wake any of the other girls.

"Yeah! What's up?" she asked in her sleepy voice.

Sgt. Reynolds stared for a moment, it was early morning, but Cookie looked radiant. Her hair was pinned back into a ponytail, she had on a white tank top and no bra support. The dorm was cold, so her nipples peeked out of her shirt like two bullets, and her boxers hugged her hips ever so tightly.

Sgt. Reynolds was one of those male officers that worked in the women's dorm to take advantage of his job whenever he could. He had been after Cookie for some time now, but she had never given him the time of day.

"That's how you talk to me?" he asked, staring at the silhouette of her breasts through her shirt. "Whatever, boy!" she huffed, shifting her body. "You woke me up."

"From the looks of it, you must have been dreaming about me," he cut in, licking his lips. "What do you want, Derek" she snapped, crossing her arms.

"You know what I want!" he responded, dropping his eyes down to her hips.

"Boy, I ain't got time to be playing with you!" she blurted as she turned to walk away.

"I'm going back to bed."

He stared for a moment watching her butt sway away, then he called back out to her. "Loveless."

She continued walking, so he called louder, waking up a few of the girls. "LOVE!"

"WHAT, DEREK!" she snapped with an attitude.

He stared at her for a few more moments, taking in her body structure. She gave him several facial expressions as if to say,

Speak damnit.

He knew he was getting a rise out of her, and as she was about to catch an attitude, he smiled and spoke.

"Pack ya stuff, sexy. Ya going home."

Cookie's eyes widened with excitement; this was completely unexpected news. She knew she was coming up for parole, but this was news words couldn't explain. Cookie ran back to her bunk excited, waking almost every girl in the dorm.

"Damn, bitch. Be the hell quiet!" Felicia, one of the bigger girls in the dorm spoke.

"A bitch trying to sleep" she continued, throwing a pillow over her face.

Keli, Cookie's bunkie noticed her excitement and asked, "What you so damn happy about?"

Cookie continued to smile as she began to pack her belongings.

"OH, MY GAWD GIRL!" Keli stated excitedly, noticing Cookie packing. "YOU GOING HOME!"

Keli, a 26-year-old white girl from Mobile, Alabama. She was the epitome of the stereotypical white girl. Blonde hair, blue eyes, short haircut, large breasts, small butt and half her body decorated with colorful tattoos and piercings. She was a former stripper, who was in jail doing five and a half because she took the charge for her former boyfriend who was running a home meth-lab.

They both began to jump around cheering happily, but the excitement was cut short when Felicia walked up.

"Hold up chic!" Keli blurted out with a confused look on her face.

"When You Made Parole! And how come you didn't tell me?"

"Yeah! How come you didn't tell us?"
Felicia cut in.

Felicia was the dorm stud, she was a mixture of swag like Queen Latifah from *Set It Off*, body like Laila Ali, with a face like Da Brat. She walked like an old-school pimp, always grabbing at her crotch area as if she had a penis. She kept her hair braided back, and she loved to say,

"Ya know what I'm saying," when she was trying to make a point. She had several women in the dorm she turned out sexually; a few of them even stabbed each other over her. Despite all of that, Felicia had been trying to turn Cookie out for years, to no avail.

3

"I didn't make parole" Cookie began as she continued packing "I haven't even seen the parole board."

She reached in her locker and grabbed her most important belongings: her letters from Tiger, claiming he was waiting for her, and they'll be married. Watching her pack, Felicia asked, "I know you ain't taking that commissary witcha, are ya?"

Cookie stared at the bag full of goodies she had just bought earlier that day. "Ya ought to leave it with ya girl, ya know what I'm saying." Felicia added trying to sound friendly.

"That's exactly what I was planning." Cookie spoke, as she reached around Felicia and handed Keli the bag full of commissary.

"I'm leaving it to my girl.

As she was saying her goodbyes, Sgt. Reynolds called out, "LOVELESS… pack it up, NOW!" Cookie looked toward the guard station and gave him a stare that could burn through metal.

"Unless you wanna stay," he chimed in, noticing her attitude look.

Cookie walked up to the officer's station where another officer escorted her to the front entrance to dress into civilian clothes and sign out. When the guards opened the front gate, Cookie felt as if this was unreal. Her excitement escalated when she looked to her left and saw Tiger standing there. He was wearing a Black fitted Tailored suit, holding a dozen long stem red roses, and a large six foot black and white panda teddy bear.

Cookie ran up to him, jumped into his arms and kissed him passionately. He held her so tight that it felt as if her bones were being crushed.

"I missed you so much, baby," Cookie stated with a trembling voice and tears in her eyes. Tiger smiled and nodded, as Cookie continued, "I can not wait to eat" she began slowly releasing her embrace. "I want pizza, hamburgers, chicken… anything with grease."

Tiger just continued to stare at her, not uttering a word. "You know what else I've been craving?" she continued with a seductive look on her face as she cut her eyes downward to Tiger's private area. "It's been a long while since she has been tampered with." She chimed in, patting on her now throbbing vagina.

"So, it's goooood and tight."

Tiger continued to smile and stare, making no comment at all.

"What's wrong, baby?" Cookie wondered, noticing Tiger wouldn't move nor talk. "Why aren't you talking?"

Cookie began to get frustrated; this was not the greeting she was expecting. This was not her Tiger. Not the one she had just done all this time for, "SAY SOMETHING," she demanded. Watching his face only smile. "YOU HAVE NOTHING TO SAY TO ME?" she blurted, now very angrily. "SAY SOMETHING, DAMNIT!"

Cookie stared for a moment in silence, then she noticed Tiger looked as if he was about to speak. "Come on, baby," Cookie anticipated. "Say it! Say it!"

Cookie leaned in closer, waiting to hear what beautiful thing Tiger was about to say. *He about to ask me to marry him, I know it. I just know it,* she thought. *Yes, Daddy, yes,* she continued in thought as Tiger finally blurted out,

"CHOW TIME!"

"What you say, baby?" Cookie asked with a dumbfounded look on her face.

"Chow time," Tiger repeated in the same tone as before.

"What do you mean, 'chow time'?" Cookie shot with an attitude. "Is this a joke? What the fuck is chow time? Is it 'cause I said I was hungry?" Tiger grabbed Cookie's shoulders, lightly shook her, and repeated, "Chow time. Wake up, Cookie; it's chow time."

Cookie slowly opened her eyes to see Keli shaking her shoulders. She lay in her bunk for a few more moments, glancing around at her surroundings. She was still in the women's facility. The whole ordeal had been a dream. While she had been replaying the court verdict and waking up to someone telling her she was being set free, it was devastating to realize that too had turned out to be only a dream. It felt so real, she thought as she sat up in her bunk. "That's that bullshit" she mumbled to herself as she got out of her bunk, opened her bunk locker, and scrambled through her mail. It had been over three years, and not one letter from Tiger. *Why hasn't he written me?* she thought, teary-eyed. *Had he moved on? Was he dead?* She pictured all types of scenarios to justify why he would do her so cold. All she hoped for was one letter.

* * *

Cookie got up and headed to the chow hall with Keli.

"Girl, you must have been having a hell of a dream last night," Keli said as they stood in line waiting for prison food. "Girl, you were tossing and turning and talking in your sleep."

Cookie remembered the dream, and even though she loved it, she hated that it wasn't reality.

"Girl, I probably was," she said, grabbing her food. She and Keli sat at the table.

"I had that dream again."

"The one you were running through the field naked, with honey all over you, and the bees were chasing you?"

"WHAT!" Cookie snapped with a confused look on her face.

"NO!"

"Oh, you talking 'bout the one where you running through the field naked with honey on you… and Felicia and Sasha chasing you," Keli added with a smirk.

"NO!" Cookie snapped, taking a sip on her bitter juice. "Wasn't no damn body chasing me!" As Cookie was about to reveal her dream, Sasha walked up.

* * *

SASHA, another stud in the dorm, was one of the older inmates, born back when a stud was known as a Bull-Dagger. Sasha had a pecan tan complexion, hair shaved into a low cut with waves atop. She wore her prison blues sagging under her butt, she always walked with her hand draped in her crotch area as if she had a penis.

In her earlier life she was married with two kids. She always felt she liked women, but her family were strict holy church goers, and pillars of the small town of Houma, Louisiana. So she kept her secret life hidden. Her husband

6

use to drink, gamble, and beat on her, but she stayed thinking it was for the children.

She eventually started using drugs to help cope with her home life. One day, she came home early from her job at UPS in the sorting department, and walked into a scene no mother should ever have to witness.

She witnessed her husband molesting their daughter, who was 9 at the time, as she cried out in pain, while their son, who was 5 at the time screamed out, "daddy stop hurting my sister."

That moment snapped something deep inside her. Sasha, without any thought, jumped on her husband, pulled out the box cutter she uses at work and stabbed him 85 times, then cut off his penis and shoved it in his mouth.

That act of Heroism got her 25 years to life. The jury and the crowd understood her reasoning, but the judge considered it overkill. Plus, it didn't help her case that the judge was her late husband's second cousin.

Sasha was coming up on year 19, with parole in six more. When she got to prison, she was able to let her hair down and be who she longed to be. It was like shooting fish in a barrel.

* * *

"You gone eat yo toast?" Sasha asked, reaching over Cookie head about to grab her toast.

"Sasha, you betta get the hell away from me girl!" Cookie snapped swatting her hand away.

Sasha stepped back setting up as if she was about to fight.

"Here, Sasha" Keli jumped in reaching out her toast to Sasha.

"You can have my toast."

"Nah," Sasha commented, swaying Keli's toast away. "I want *this* Bitch toast."

Other inmates started looking on seeing that it was about to be a brawl.

"Well Bitch, Ya ain't getting my toast," Cookie snapped, as she stood up to face Sasha.

Sasha was two times Cookie's size, but what Cookie lacked in size she got back in heart. "Now, you may wanna get the hell out my face and from around our table before I make you toast," Cookie huffed.

Sasha gave a devilish smile as she started cracking her knuckles. "I been waiting for this day," Sasha spoke loosening up her body. "Its on now, Bitch!"

As she and Cookie stepped towards each other to start the day off right, a loud whistle blew."Yall break up whatever it is over there," one of the officers cut in, that was guarding the exit door.

"And Sasha why you still in here anyway? Your POD been left," The officer continued.

"This ain't over, fish." Sasha spoke, slowly walking toward the exit.

"For your safety, I hope it is." Cookie snapped, as Sasha left the building.

"Sasha always trying to bully people." Keli spoke upset.

"Well, she picked the right one today." Cookie interjected as they stood up, dumped their trays and lined up to return to their dorms.

"So, what were you saying about your dream?" Keli asked, trailing behind Cookie as they walked.

"It was the one about Tiger" Cookie responded."Your man, Tiger?" Keli asked surprised.

"No! My pet Tiger." Cookie responded sarcastically.

"Of course, my man Tiger, who else would I be referring to?"

"So, you done heard from him yet?" Keli asked as she was about to climb in her bunk to get a few more moments of sleep before they do work call.

"NO!" Cookie responded, shaking her head depressed.

"It's been over 3 years, baby." Keli cut in, removing her jumpsuit, as she continued, "Don't you think it's bout time for you to stop calling him your man?"

Cookie couldn't respond. That statement hit her hard. Had she been hanging on to a dream? What kept her going was, in her mind; when this was all over, her and Tiger would have that fairy tale life she'd always dreamed of. The life she felt they had when she was free. The thought weighed heavy on her heart. She laid back on her bunk, covers pulled to her face, and quietly cried herself to sleep.

* * *

"WORK CALL!" Sgt. Reynolds yelled out.

It was 8 a.m., time for the ladies to pay down their debt to society. Cookie opened her eyes but laid there momentarily. Keli jumped out of the top bunk with an excited look on her face.

"Come on, chic," she said, shaking Cookie playfully. "It's time to make the donuts."

"No! It's time to go back to sleep," Cookie quickly responded, turning her body away from Keli, who continued to tug on her.

"LOVELESS!" Sgt. Reynolds called out, motioning for her to come to the officer's station.

"What, Derek?" she asked with a tired, irritated voice.

You don't plan on reporting to work call?" he asked, taking a sip of his coffee that he spikes with vodka.

When Cookie was about to speak, Mesha, aka Cream, walked by. A former stripper from Tallahassee, she was doing five years for assault with a deadly weapon and afflicting bodily harm. She had cut a few of the girls across the face with her razor when they attempted to jump her after finding out she slept with their men.

Cream walked by, with her work suit in her hand. Sgt. Reynolds noticed she was wearing only underwear and her sports bra. His eyes were glued to her butt until she vanished into the shower area.

"HELLOOOOOO!" Cookie chimed in, snapping him out of his trance.

"What?" he responded, laughing playfully, forgetting what he even wanted Cookie for.

"You nasty," Cookie said, as she began to walk off with a disgusted look on her face.

"You about to be released." Reynolds blurted.

Cookie's breathing level increased; this was just like her dream this morning. Without turning to face Reynolds, Cookie calmly asked, "You say I'm 'bout to be released?"

"Well, not released-released," he corrected quickly. "I just saw you have a

9

parole hearing Tuesday."

To Cookie, that information was just as exciting as an immediate release. She quickly got dressed and reported to work call. She couldn't wait to tell Keli her news.

* * *

Cookie and Keli were both put on trash detail. Felicia and her goon squad got themselves placed on it too after a little manipulation of the guard.

Felicia was trying to stay near Cookie; she felt one day Cookie would crumble or get caught in a dark corner, and that's when she'd bite. "I see Mr. Ma'am and her band of Merry Men got put on our work detail also," Keli said, noticing Felicia and her crew.

Cookie looked back and caught eyes with Felicia, who was making a lot of sexual gestures with her tongue and fingers.

Keli and Cookie laughed hysterically.

"What's so funny?" Felicia asked as she quickly walked up between them. Keli began picking up trash while Cookie was changing the bags out of the cans.

"Come on, ladies, make me laugh," Felicia persisted. "I like to laugh too."

Keli stood up, holding trash, and blurted, "Unfortunately, I left my mirror in the dorm so we could show you what we laughing at."

Cookie laughed even harder.

Felicia quickly turned her attention toward Cookie, who wasn't fazed at Felicia's gaze.

"You just a little Ms. Giggle Box, aren't ya, J-Ville?" She slowly circled around Cookie, licking her lips, then returned her attention to Keli — who was watching, ready to fight with her girl if she needed to.

"So, that was supposed to be a joke?" Felicia began. "You a lil comedian, huh, snowflake?""Nah," Cookie cut in quickly.

"That was just a lil inside thang from earlier."She attempted to cut the tension, but Felicia was on go-mode.

"Inside thang, huh?" Felicia repeated, turning her attention back to Cookie. "I loooove to be inside thangs."

Felicia stretched out her tongue, showing it could reach below her chin.

"Oooookay," Cookie said, wide-eyed. "Well, good *lick* with that... I mean, good luck. Good LUCK with that."

Cookie quickly picked up her garbage bags, and she and Keli walked away.

When Cookie and Keli got a nice distance away from Felicia and her team, Cookie turned to Keli and said, "She really believes she a man, don't she?"

Keli looked back to see Felicia still eyeing Cookie.

"Felicia gonna take your goodies," Keli joked. "The devil is a liar," Cookie cut in quickly. "She ain't getting nowhere near my goodies."

"It ain't all that bad," Keli commented in a low tone.

"I'm just saying, she ain't..." Cookie stopped in the middle of her sentence, realizing what Keli said. "What ain't all that bad?"

Keli looked up, then turned her eyes away, blushing.

"UUUUGHH!" Cookie began laughing.

"You carpet muncher."

"Now that's a lie," Keli snapped.

"I didn't do her. She did me."

"So, you saying..." Cookie started as she began throwing the bags in the dumpster.

"She ate you out, and not once did she ask you to do her?"

"That's exactly what I'm saying," Keli defended as she continued. "I guess she get off just doing you."

Cookie's face crumbled up with a half-smile, half-frown look.

"Uuuuugh," Cookie laughed jokingly.

"You a lesbo now."

"What the fuck is a lesbo?" Keli wondered.

"A lesbo," Cookie repeated. "A lesbian."

Cookie laughed as she playfully hugged Keli, who wasn't laughing.

"I ain't no damn lesbian," Keli snapped, trying to hold back laughter as Cookie kept mimicking the scissor sign with her hand.

"You joking," Keli continued.

"But did you see the size of that bitch's tongue? I know some dicks that's not that long."

11

"I don't know who you been fucking," Cookie mumbled under her breath.

"What you say?" Keli asked curiously.

"Oh, nothing," Cookie lied. "Just thinking out loud."

"But this was years ago," Keli said, seeming to be reminiscing.

"How many times?" Cookie asked.

"ONCE!" Keli quickly snapped back, checking Cookie's facial expression.

Cookie felt if it was once, given the circumstances, once wasn't that bad.

There was a brief silence as they were changing the bags out of the warehouse garbage cans. Keli glanced up at Cookie, and with an embarrassed look on her face, she said,

"Four times."

2

Blood on the Track

It was the weekend, so there was no work call. Cookie was up using the bathroom when she noticed Keli in the TV room watching Hannah Montana. She was one of the few waiting around for the officers to unlock the dorm doors so they could go outside for recreation.

"I was meaning to ask you," Cookie began, stepping into the TV room. "You watch this show faithfully every Saturday. What's up with that?"

Keli paused for a moment, lowered her head, and said, "Well, it's like this..." She began trying to hold back tears. "My daughter was three years old when I came in here, and every Saturday we used to watch it together." She wiped a tear away as she finished.

"She used to call her 'Nanna Nontana.'"

Cookie watched as Keli gazed into thought. "Where's your daughter now?" Cookie asked in a sympathetic voice.

"She's with my mom in Texas," Keli responded, turning her attention back toward the TV.

"Is that the daughter that—?"

"Yeah, that's her," Keli cut in, not letting Cookie finish her statement.

* * *

Three years ago, Keli and her daughter Hannah drove to her then-boyfriend's

13

house. She had received intel from some of the girls at the club that her boyfriend was sleeping with someone near where he did his pharmaceutical business.

She and Hannah walked inside the house. No one was there. Keli noticed bundles of money and drugs on the counter. She began stuffing her purse, and when it was full, she stuffed her daughter's bag. Without warning, there was a loud bam on the door.

The police yelled.

Then the door flung open.

She could hear the footsteps approaching fast, but she couldn't empty her purse quickly enough. By the time she tried to grab her daughter and escape, several cops were already on them, guns drawn.

She refused to turn in her boyfriend or testify against him. Because she wouldn't cooperate, the state had DCF take her daughter, charged Keli with the drugs, and sent her to prison for five and a half years. Eventually, her mom was able to gain custody.

To add insult to injury, her then-boyfriend broke up with her, claiming she was toxic and bad for his life.

Keli was overjoyed when she later found out her ex and the girl he'd been cheating with were both killed in a home invasion. As karma would have it, the girl's boyfriend, a rival meth dealer, hired some jits to break into the house and "handle" him. Coincidentally, the girl was there that night. Guns were drawn. Shots were fired. They both died from multiple gunshot wounds.

* * *

Cookie placed her arms around Keli, who was no longer able to hold back tears.

"REC CALL! REC CALL!" Officer Stevens yelled through the intercom.

"Everybody that's going outside to rec, come line up by the exit."

Almost all the girls in the dorm lined up for rec. "Come on, Snowflake," Cookie joked, helping Keli off the bench.

"Let's go outside and get some fresh air."

* * *

"There them bitches go right there," Sasha commented to Felicia as they watched Cookie and Keli walk the dirt track.

Felicia watched Cookie with lustful eyes, while Sasha watched her with the kind of vengeance still simmering from what happened in the cafeteria earlier that week.

"That bitch gotta run me the fade," Sasha said, jumping around excitedly.

"And I *dare* that lil white bitch to jump in. I'ma tear her ass a new one."

"Hold off there, Sash," Felicia chimed in as she racked up the book she'd just won playing spades.

"I don't want her face too fucked up. I still ain't hit that yet."

Felicia played another card, and one of the girls at the table stood up and screamed:

"YOU RENEGED!"

Felicia paused mid-conversation with Sasha and turned to the girl.

"I did what, bitch?" she huffed, clenching her cards into a fist.

"I said you reneged,"

the girl repeated confidently.

"You cut my *King of Clubs* earlier, then you just played the nine of clubs," the girl, who had only been locked up almost six months, stated excitedly.

"Let us get them three books out ya," she said, starting to twerk in her seat like she'd accomplished something.

But her partner knew better.

She saw the renege.

She knew she could prove it.

But she also knew she'd be a damn fool to call Felicia out on it.

"Show me which book it is," Felicia said, leaning back in her chair with her fist still planted on the table.

"This book right here," the girl said.

As she leaned over the table to reveal the *"mysterious"* book, she never saw Felicia reach back and swing forward with everything she had.

The girl hit the deck with extreme force.

Not one person made a sound.

Not one person alerted the C.O.

"Fuck your king of clubs, bitch," Felicia snapped, standing over her.

"You just got hit by the Queen of Clubs."

She threw the remainder of her cards on top of the unconscious girl, then stood up, prepared to walk away.

"I want my cigarettes and my soups,"

Felicia demanded to the girl's partner.

"I consider this a forfeit for y'all."

Felicia and Sasha walked to the edge of the covered porch as they continued watching Keli and Cookie walk.

"Whatever you gonna do, you better do it fast," Sasha began.

"Word on the pound, ya girl Cookie go before the parole board Tuesday."

Felicia's eyes widened as Sasha continued.

"And it's a damn good chance she gonna get it.

Felicia no longer watched Cookie with lustful eyes. Her whole demeanor shifted into something darker as she responded,

"Not if I have anything to do with it."

* * *

"So, Tuesday the big day, huh?" Keli chimed in as Cookie's face lit up.

"And it is!" Cookie responded, sassy. "And girl, I can't wait."

"Don't get out there and forget about ya girl," Keli said sadly.

"Aww." Cookie and Keli hugged.

"You my girl for life."

While they were talking, they didn't see Felicia, Sasha, and her crew run out onto the track toward them. One of the girls with Felicia immediately stuck Keli in the side with an unidentified shank.

"FUUUUCK!" Keli yelled out as she fell to the ground, clutching her ribs.

When Cookie turned to react, Sasha stepped in front of her.

"What's up wit it now!" Sasha demanded, swinging at Cookie. Cookie dodged the blow and immediately came back with blow after blow. She was too busy

16

playing defense to land anything solid.

Sasha pulled out a blade she had hidden in her boxers and swung fast, slicing Cookie across the forearm. When she raised her hand to strike again, the yard alarm went off — giving Cookie the break she needed. Cookie grabbed Sasha's wrist, snatched the blade from her hand, and drove it into Sasha's abdomen.

Sasha clutched her stomach and dropped to her knees.

Officers rushed in from every direction, yelling commands. Everything was happening so fast Cookie went deaf to the noise. Several officers tackled her, forcing her face into the dirt as they pried the knife from her hand.

From the ground, she turned her head just enough to see Keli lying on her back, eyes wide open.

Lifeless.

When they stood Cookie up, along with the other girls from Felicia's clique, she caught eyes with Felicia.

There was a devilish grin on her face.

Cookie felt it instantly: this was a setup. And her parole hearing was only days away.

As the guards marched them toward confinement, Felicia walked by and said:

"What a bummer. I guess you won't be going home Tuesday after all."

* * *

Sunday and Monday were bad days for Cookie. All she thought about was Keli lying on the ground. *Was she dead? What would happen tomorrow? How would the board treat this situation?* If she didn't get this parole accepted, she would be obligated to do the whole eight years. *It was self-defense,* she thought to herself, staring at the ceiling in her 6 by 9 concrete confined space.

She curled up in a ball, then turned to face the wall so no one would see her crying if they walked in.

Her mind drifted to visions of Tiger and all the great times they had. But her heart hardened at the thought that he had abandoned her. It had been over three years and not one piece of mail. If he wasn't dead, he was going to be when she got out. The stress was so unbearable that she hadn't eaten in 2 days.

She had made up her mind that if she did have to max out because of the trick Felicia and her team pulled, she would make them wish they were dead.

Cookie forced herself to sleep once again. She was ready to see what tomorrow would bring at the parole hearing.

* * *

TUESDAY AFTERNOON, 12:45 P.M.
PAROLE BOARD HEARING

"Have a seat," the lady from the parole board stated as Cookie walked in the door nervously."Inmate 12677, Serena Loveless," Mr. Parker, the head parole officer, began.

"You were convicted of conspiracy to the possession of a controlled substance with the intent to sell, and were sentenced to eight years, with parole eligibility after three and a half."

He glanced at her file, looked up at her, then continued, "You have completed forty-two months of an eight-year sentence."

He glanced down at the file again, then back at her. "Up until a few days ago, you didn't have as much as a warning on your file. Now you and several other inmates may be facing charges of assault with a deadly weapon."

Cookies heart began to beat out her chest, she could see the rejection stamp already on her file."You are aware that one of the girls died from her wounds, so; someone is going to have a murder charge added to there docket."

She watched as her life was being decided by an older white woman and two older white men, who looked as if they were present when Martin Luther King marched and they were the ones spraying them with the fire hoses and siccing the dogs on them.

Now, she was sure they were about to find a way to plant this Murder on her, somehow. "Before we present our decision; do you have anything you would like us to consider." Mr. Parker asked, closing her file and placing it before himself for stamp confirmation.

Cookie thought long and hard, they didn't want to hear what happened outside that day, as far as they were concerned, they all were guilty. She had to think.

Then her mind got an idea.

The Shawshank Redemption. Red kept getting denied, until he took account-ability and not beg for freedom, but accept whatever was to come.

She began with, "There is no excuse for what went on the other day, and although its unfortunate that people got hurt, however———"

"No, someone died!" Ms. Stevens, the female parole officer chimed in, with a snappy tone. Cookie nodded in confirmation as she continued.

"My condolences to the family of the deceased, but that's almost everyday in here."

She glanced over the judges panel and felt her speech was falling on deaf ears.

"Its like crabs in a barrel in here. No one wants to see you leave unless its them. You are lucky if u wake up, let alone get to go home. We are constantly being molested, Harassed, beat, and cut." She showed her forearm with the cut from the fight the other day.

"Its so much we have to endure in here. And I have done my Damnest to make it this far in this Hell hole."

She held her hands up in praise, looked up to the heavens and testified, "It's only by the grace of God that I made it this far without an infraction. Cause with the girls that's in here." She paused.

"The staff." She paused again then looked around the room at the officers present at the hearing.

"And the food." She brought her hands down to her knees, shook her head and added, "I would have killed someone a long time ago."

The judges all shifted their bodies. Now paying attention.

"It was also the thought of jumping into the arms of my husband when I leave these gates.""Your files never said you were married." Mr. Parker stated, again skimming through her file."Not quite yet." Cookie began.

"But the moment you approve my Parole and let me out that gate. The next time you read anything about me, its gonna be in a newspaper broadcasting my wedding day."

Cookie sat back in her chair, felt like she had said enough.

The parole board mumbled amongst each other for minutes which seemed like forever to Cookie.

The suspense was deafening, even the escort officer was anticipating the response.

"Ms. Loveless?" the head parole officer began."It's not often that I'm given a situation like yours where everything says deny, deny, deny..."

(Short pause)

"...and yet I feel that would be a travesty to justice."

Cookie raised her head up, heart still pounding, but this time from excitement, as she heard the officer say:

"We have unanimously decided to approve your parole."

Cookie clasped her hands together as tears of joy streamed down her face.

"Thank u. Thank u. Thank u. Thank u. Thank u," she kept repeating, rocking back and forth in her chair.

"Don't thank me yet," Mr. Parker continued.

"I'm requesting there be a six-month conditional probationary unsupervised monitoring."

Cookie nodded in agreement while he continued:

"In that time, I expect you to have a job, and show the ability to maintain said job. Do I make myself clear?"

"Crystal clear."

"Well, with that being said, I wish you the best. Have a good day."

Cookie was so excited, she turned, ran, and jumped into Sgt. Reynolds' arms.

When she realized what she had done, she eased away and tried to calm her composure.

"My bad," she said, feeling embarrassed.

"It's all good," he chimed in. "I understand."

"I can't wait to tell Keli," Cookie added, feeling that the girl who died was Sasha, being that her stabbing was worse.

"About Keli…"

Sgt. Reynolds began with a soft voice.

Cookie could tell from his facial expression his news wouldn't be good.

"Noooooo!"

Cookie screamed out, backing away.

"Not my girl. Not my girl. NOT MY GIRL!"

"I'm sorry," Sgt. Reynolds responded, standing there.

After a few moments of uncontrollable tears, Cookie's thoughts of vengeance overshadowed the news she had just received moments ago. Felicia, and everyone involved, must die, she thought while being escorted back to her dorm.

However, she wasn't about to risk being released and giving Felicia what she wanted. She felt she would be more powerful pulling strings from the outside.

"I see we were able to convince the board to grant your parole regardless of my witness statement," Felicia stated from across the dorm while she watched Cookie pack.

No response from Cookie. She kept glancing up at Keli's empty bunk.

"She ain't coming back," Felicia cut in, noticing Cookie's gaze.

"But like 80 percent of the girls in the system, you'll be back."

Cookie stood up, having packed all her belongings and rolled up her bunk. While walking toward the exit, Felicia added: "And I'll be waiting."

* * *

Cookie was expecting to be escorted to the bus station. She was told by the exit officers she had a ride waiting outside for her.

Tiger, she thought. A deep smile came across her face. All the time he wasn't there was about to be forgiven just that fast. All was better.

She took the $1,245 check they gave her from what was left in her commissary and headed toward the exit.

Her heart was pounding from excitement when she saw a white Mercedes E-Class with 22-inch white Forgiato rims, tires, and extremely dark tint.

I love him so much, she mumbled as the prison gates slowly opened. She ran out the gate toward the car, yet slowed down when Tiger never got out.

She hesitated. She couldn't see inside the car and was not about to open that door without knowing who was inside.

"Baby, get out the car," Cookie said, squinting her eyes, trying to get a glimpse.

Cookie saw the driver's side door open slowly. She bounced with excitement at the vision of Tiger's face.

When the driver exited the vehicle, Cookie was surprised and blurted out—"Big Lez?"

3

Brotherly Love

"Why are you here instead of Tiger?" Cookie asked, immediately sitting inside Lez's Benz. "Well, hello to you too," Lez stated sarcastically, driving out of the prison parking lot.

"My bad." Cookie leaned back, took a few deep breaths, then responded, "It's been a hell of a ride lately."

"I can imagine," Lez chimed in. "Well, ya look good as ever. Body still banging."

Lez continued glancing over at Cookie, who was adjusting the bandage on her arm.

"What happened to ya arm?"

Cookie glanced down at her arm, reminiscing on the events from just days ago.

"Some lil' stud bitches called themselves jumping me and my homegirl."

"JUMPED Y'ALL?" Lez snapped.

"And that bitch cut you?!"

Big Lez got so amped up she almost ran off the road into another car.

"I'ma need you to keep your eyes on the road, Miss Ma'am," Cookie commented, finally putting her seatbelt on.

"I'm good over here. This is definitely not over." "It sure as hell better not be!" Lez cut in.

Cookie added, "I'm for damn sure gonna get my lick back."

* * *

Four hours later, they finally pulled up to Big Lez's house in Queens Harbor. Luxury houses in the Southside Beach area of Jacksonville.

Cookie had slept the last two hours of the ride home. She woke up to Lez pulling into her secured neighborhood — acres upon acres of million-dollar luxury homes. Doctors, lawyers, pro-athletes, tycoons. The top elite.

Cookie glanced over at Lez and watched as she pulled up to a large black manor-style fence that opened from a button in her car.

"Where the hell you got me at, girl?" Cookie asked, looking at the massive mansion with a circular driveway and a waterfall sculpture of a half-naked lady wearing a crown.

"This my home," Lez said calmly, pulling up to the front entrance.

A middle-aged man wearing a butler-style suit stood waiting. There were ten steps leading up to the front doors. At the bottom of the steps, on each side, were two white sculpted lions, also wearing crowns and holding scepters in their paws as if they were guards for the Queen of England.

"Who all stay in this big ass house with you?" Cookie asked, amazed.

"Just me and my staff."

"STAFF!" Cookie yelled out excitedly.

"Yeah, staff," Lez reiterated. "Who else gonna keep this place clean?"

"Welcome home, madam," the butler stated, greeting Lez.

"I had the guest room prepared, just as you asked."

"Thank you, Timothy," Lez responded in her proper voice as they stood on the bottom step talking with him.

"Could you have Mary run me and my girl a bath? It's been a long ride and I'm sweaty."

"Very well, ma'am," Timothy responded and trotted upstairs to the massive double doors that led into Lez's house.

"This is…" Cookie paused, taking it all in. "INCREDIBLE!"

"Why thank you," Lez began. "10,000 sq. ft. Six bedrooms. Five bath. Game room. Movie room. Workout room. Heated pool, and a massage room."

"Will that be all, madam?" Timothy asked, waiting for orders.

"Could you get Michael to prepare us a lunch? We'll have it by the back garden."

Timothy nodded as Lez continued.

"And could you also make sure Mary puts my special bubble beads in there this time? Last time she forgot."

"Very well, ma'am," Timothy responded, then walked off.

"Giiiiiirl, who are you?" Cookie joked, watching Timothy translate what Lez asked to Mary, the Spanish housemaid.

"Girl, I'm HER!" Lez snapped.

"I KNOW THAT'S RIGHT!" Cookie snapped back as they both laughed.

"You talkin' all proper and shit," Cookie started. "You all like, 'Timothy, run me a bath. Prepare us a lunch… in the garden.'"

Cookie paused for a second.

"Bitch, you got a garden."

Lez laughed.

"The Lez I know would have said, 'Aye cuz, get the maid to go run me some water. Put some Dawn in it to make some bubbles. Have Mike cook us suttin' to eat and put it by the flowers outside.'"

"Really, bitch?" Lez responded with a blushy smile. "I'm not that damn ghetto."

"Oh yes… you are," Cookie snapped.

Lez stared off for a moment.

"That's how I have to act in this neighborhood."(Slight pause.)

"No one would take me seriously if I acted otherwise. They respect Big Lez from Ken Knight. No one would fear Leslie Hill from Queens Harbor."

Cookie nodded in understanding.

"You familiar with the street me. This the home me."

They both began to walk upstairs.

"Now let me show you to your room."

Walking up the circular staircase to the second floor, they stopped outside Cookie's guest room. Cookie turned toward Lez and said,"I like this side of you. This the Lez I can get to know."

Lez smiled, stared for a moment, then walked to her room.

* * *

After the long bubble bath and lunch, Cookie decided to take a nap on her California king-size pillow-top mattress. The bed was built for royalty, large pillars on each corner and lace drapes trimmed around the top. It was totally different from what she slept on the last few years in the correctional facility.

Her dream took her back to the day when she and Tiger were on the run. Police cars, helicopters, and Det. Holzendorf were all after them. The horrible playback of her taking a bullet in her top shoulder before her and Tiger could make it to the last fence that would have gotten them out the neighborhood. She envisioned Tiger holding her closely as she felt as if her life was being taken from her body. She listened as Tiger confessed his love for her before blacking out from loss of blood.

She remembered waking up in Shands Hospital, handcuffed to a bed, with an IV and tubes going through several parts of her body as they were giving her blood to replace what she lost. She remembered officers stationed outside her room, and no one was allowed in or out. Detective Holzendorf constantly came to harass her about the whereabouts of Tiger. She was given the option to help them find out where he was located, and she could possibly go free. She refused to help in any form or fashion and was charged with participation in a drug ring.

Cookie was woken up with Lez hovering over her.

"Girl," Cookie started with a startled look on her face. "What the hell are you doing?"

"Come ride with me!" Lez responded with an excited tone.

"Ride with you where?" Cookie asked in a pouty voice, turning her back on Lez, attempting to go back to sleep.

"Gotta make a couple runs. Go pick up some money from some people."

"Oh, hell nah!" Cookie snapped. "I just got out behind some shit like this." She threw the cover over her shoulder and continued, "I'll pass." "Come ooooooon," Lez pleaded, shaking Cookie profusely. "We can make it a girl's

26

day. Mani-pedi's. Massages."

Cookie slid the cover down, and glanced over her shoulder toward lez who was flashing a credit card.

Cookie slid the cover down and glanced over her shoulder toward Lez, who was flashing a credit card.

"And then we can go shoppiiiiinnnng."

"Why didn't you start with that?" Cookie responded, throwing her covers off her.

* * *

Lounging back in a recliner chair with facial cream and cucumber on their faces, Cookie decided to pick Lez's brain.

"Leslie?" Cookie began after she took a sip of her lemon water.

"Yeah," Lez responded, enjoying her hand massage from the attendants at the spa.

"Why I never seen you with no dude?"

"Cause men ain't shit!" she snapped quickly.

Cookie sat up and removed the cucumber from her eye.

"Girl, I'm serious."

"So am I!" Lez snapped back quickly.(Uncomfortable pause)

Lez sat up, removed her cucumber, and asked, "Am I lying?"

"So, you never met a guy that you felt was worth your time?" Cookie asked curiously.

"Most these niggas just good for one thang, girl. And half of them can't do that right."

"So, you use guys for sex and money?" Cookie continued.

"Absolutely NOT!" Lez snapped. "Shit, I got my own money. Plus, I got toys that can get me off better than half these dudes can."

"So, you done swore off men?" Cookie inquired.

"Not entirely," Lez responded, directing the attendants to massage her calves and feet.

"It just feels weird dating or fucking a dude that has significantly less than you."

"So, you don't have at least one guy friend you call to help get you off? You just use toys every time you in the mood?"

"Nah," Lez answered slowly as she envisioned Tiger. "I have a friend who get me off right."

"See, there ya go," Cookie stated. "Who is it? Is he from the neighborhood?" Lez nodded in agreement.

"Just a really, really good friend," Lez spoke with a smile.

"Aaaawwwww. He got you blushing. He must be special."

"He definitely is," Lez confirmed. "But it could never be."

"WHY!" Cookie snapped quickly.

Lez looked deeply into Cookie's eyes with light sympathy and stated, "He in a relationship."

"Ooooooooh." Cookie started, thought for a moment, then added, "Fuck that hoe."

"Nah. It ain't that type of party," Lez spoke with a light laugh. "Any other time it would have been 'fuck that hoe,' but this one a lil different."

Cookie rolled her eyes at Lez, then leaned back into her recliner and placed her cucumbers back on her eyes.

Lez noticed the shift and asked, "What was that?"

"Nothing," Cookie said sarcastically.

"Ain't no nothing!" Lez snapped back. "If we gonna talk about it, let's talk about it."

Cookie sat up quickly; the cucumbers fell from her eyes as she began, "I picked you as a woman who, when she sees something she wants, she go and gets it."

She called the attendants back to where she was and asked for more cucumbers.

"But I could be mistaken. I have been wrong before."

"It's not like you think it is," Lez stated with a defeated tone in her voice.

"Like I said," Cookie began, grabbing the new cucumbers from the attendant. She leaned back in the recliner, placed them on her eyes, and repeated, "I have been wrong before."

* * *

Lez and Cookie had a very relaxing day. Full spa treatment, massage, nails, and shopping; and not once had she asked about Tiger. Cookie had it in her mind that Tiger put Lez up to all this wine, dine, and pampering. In her mind, he wanted her to get beautified, then he would show up later to whisk her off into the sunset to make up for three and a half years.

She would play along. So far, according to what she saw right now, he was off to a great start.

Lez and Cookie pulled up to Picketville — a rival territory of Washington Heights and Ken Knight, Lez's stomping grounds.

"Damn, Lez!" Josh blurted as Lez stepped out of her car and walked up to him.

"You get finer every time I see ya."

"Well, I know one thang," Lez began with a Kool-Aid smile on her face.

"Nobody can't ever accuse you of being blind."

It was early afternoon; the sun was out; Lez had on a blue one-piece romper bodysuit that hugged her body perfectly. Her butt danced like a soundtrack was playing every move she made.

Her back was out, and her nipples were demanding attention. The diamond choker and bracelets she wore glistened every time she moved. And to accent the whole ensemble, on her feet were a fresh pair of French-Blue Retro Air Jordan 12s.

"Speaking of someone being blind…" Lez began, noticing Josh's continuous stare at her.

"Why I don't SEE my money in front of me?"

"Oh, shit." Josh snapped out of his trance. "I gotcha, ma."

Josh walked into the house to retrieve Lez's money. He was indebted to her for one hundred thousand dollars. She could vaguely hear him on the phone talking with someone, confirming she was there. This didn't seem like a setup because he already owed her, nothing more to gain but she was gonna be cautious either way.

He had been in the house for over 15 minutes. This was definitely a stall tactic.

She walked back to her car where she knew she had a couple guns. With the outfit she had on, it would be hard to conceal it.

She discussed the situation with Cookie, and Cookie agreed to be her wingman.

Cookie grabbed Lez's pink and chrome 9mm from out of the glove compartment, stepped out, and stood next to Lez. "Daaaaaamn," Josh blurted, noticing Cookie when he came outside holding a small bookbag.

"Is all the bitches you hang with fine!"

"Call her a bitch again, and you gonna find out in the worst way possible."

"My bad, Lez," Josh pleaded, throwing his hands up in surrender. "I choose peace."

"Just verify my money so I can go, man."

"About that..." Josh started. "I'm a lil short."

Lez let out a heavy sigh as she reached for the bookbag.

"I don't do well with shorts," she snapped, looking inside the bag and pulling out one of the bundles.

"What the fuck is this?" she asked, fumbling through the bag. "Where the hell is the rest of my money?"

"That's sixty-five," Josh stated, pointing at the bag. "I just need a few more days. A few of my people had a lil trouble cooking the dope!""THAT'S BULLSHIT!" Lez snapped, about to reach for her gun.

Cookie gave a sarcastic smirk, then headed back to the car. She felt Lez had this under control.

"My coke is the best, in and outside the city. It damn near sells itself."

As Lez was making her point, Josh could clearly see she was about to reach one thousand on the anger scale. Just then, a blue Dodge Hellcat pulled up. The driver revved the engine loudly, sounding like 30 lions roaring at once. His tint was dark, but Lez knew she had seen that car somewhere before.

Lez stared for a short moment to see if the driver would exit. Her mind was brought back to the present when Josh responded, "This one of the guys right here who owe me money."

Lez once again turned toward the Hellcat, and this time the door opened.

She could see a silhouette of a guy but not the clear image.

"Well, go get my money," she spoke softly but stern.

Josh waved for the guy in the car to walk over to him and Lez.

"You ain't got nothing on ya, do ya?" Josh asked, catching Lez's attention.

"Nigga, what!" she snapped, with a confused yet serious look on her face.

"He wanted to get a half a brick too," Josh added. "Boy!" Lez started with an attitude. "You betta just———."

"Well, well, well," the unidentified guy began, cutting Lez off mid-sentence as he walked up on Josh and her with a sarcastic smirk on his face. "If it ain't the infamous Big Lez."

Lez stared at him with a confused look. He knew her apparently, but she had no idea who he was.

"Do I know you?" she asked, watching his devilish grin.

"Nah, not quite," he stated softly. "But you definitely knew my brother."

"Who is your brother?" Lez wondered.

"Who you talking 'bout? Eric?" Josh asked. "ERIC!" Lez snapped. "I don't know any Erics."

She turned back to Josh.

"Wzup with my money?"

"Yeah, Eric," he confirmed. "He talked about you all the time. Big Lez this, Big Lez that."

"Like I said, whoever you are..." Lez turned back again, this time getting very agitated.

"I don't know no Erics."

"Well, he's dead now anyway," he continued, still being persistent.

"Sorry to hear that. Now about my money!" Lez jumped back on Josh.

Before Josh could respond, the unidentified visitor added,

"You probably knew him as E-Man."

Lez froze.

E-Man was the one guy who got Lez to lower her guards and love a little. However, one day when she and E-Man were lying together, Tiger called and needed her to handle something for him. E-Man didn't like the way his girl jumped when another guy spoke. He and Tiger had some heated words, and

Lez had a quick decision to make: side with the guy who loved her and who she could see herself with in another life, or the guy she loves who gave her the game and created Big Lez.

She shot and killed Eric to prove loyalty to Tiger. And she regretted it ever since.

"You E-Man's brother?"

"I'm E-Man's brother," he cut in quickly, staring hard at Lez, watching her slow, nervous movement.

"So E was fuckin' Lez, huh?" Josh joked.

"They ever found out who killed him?" Josh questioned.

"I *know* who killed him!" he snapped in a stern tone. "I've always known."

He continued to stare at Lez, eyes blaring. Frozen stance.

"WHO!" Josh asked, surprised.

"The Queen herself," he stated, pointing at Lez. "WHAT THE FUCK!" Josh snapped, surprised.

"I know you lying."

"Ask her am I lying," he added softly, yet in a devilish voice.

Josh glanced over at Lez, waiting for a response. Her and Eric's brother were exchanging stares.

She finally spoke.

"I have no idea what you are talking about," Lez lied.

"Listen, shawty," Eric's brother cut in, reminiscing about that night.

"The day my brother died, he called me. He had gotten a quarter brick from you that was for me. When I got there, I could hear y'all in the room fucking. Then shortly after, I heard him and some dude arguing on the phone."

Josh was all ears as Eric's brother continued. Lez glanced over at the car toward Cookie and gave her the signal that things had taken a turn for the worse.

"I didn't think nothing of it at first." He continued. "But then, I heard gun shots, then silence."

Lez could remember that night precisely. It haunted her ever since.

"I didn't have my gun, so I hid" he spoke then continued. "Then I watched you come out the room carrying my brothers' chain."

He glanced over at Lez and shook his head."What's crazy is, I remember seeing you turn back toward the room and telling my brother to call you later on, so I'm thinking maybe he okay. But I ran in there after you left, and he was lying across the bed in a pool of his blood... dead.""OOOOOOHH shit." Josh chimed in.

"And I knew then, you were a crazy Bitch.

And I vowed to find you and kill you myself."

Lez turned back toward her car again to see where the hell was Cookie, but she was not in the car.

I know this bitch aint run and leave me for dead." She thought. *"What the fuck Tiger saw in this spooky ass hoe."*

"I will admit," Eric's brother started, "you weren't easy to find. Nobody knew shit about you — or weren't talking."

Lez watched as Eric's brother pulled out his gun and cocked it.

"Whoa, whoa, whoa!" Josh pleaded.

"The fuck you doing, man?"

"Ending this bitch today," he added. "It took me years to find this hoe. And when you called and told me you had someone with that work, and it was her? It was perfect."

"Come on, Tank, don't do this shit, dawg," Josh pleaded. "Not here anyway. You gonna have my shit hot as fuck."

"Fuck that, Josh," Tank began.

"THIS HOE AIN'T SEEING ANOTHER DAY."

Tank raised his gun, pointed it at Lez's face. She tensed up, squeezed her eyes tightly, anticipating her life to end.

"Tell my brother I said wzup."

POW! POW!

4

Run Me My Money

"WHAT THE FUCK, MAN!" Josh pleaded in a panic. "HOW THE FUCK AM I GONNA EXPLAIN THIS SHIT!"

He glanced up and down the street to see if anyone had seen or heard the shots. He had several old and nosey neighbors.

"Police 'bout to be all over my shit now. Fuuuuuuuck," he spat as he ran into the house to move all his drug paraphernalia.

Lez peeked through one eye. She didn't make any sudden movements as she slowly glanced around her surroundings. If this was what being shot felt like, it didn't hurt much. *Am I dead?* she thought. *Is this purgatory?* This *definitely* wasn't Heaven.

She assumed she would see Hell hounds meet her and drag her to Satan so he could thank her for all the souls she brought him.

She fully opened both eyes slowly to see Cookie standing over Tank's lifeless body. "BIIIIIITCH!" Lez blurted happily. "I thought you ditched my ass."

Cookie was so traumatized holding Lez's gun that her body had frozen. She began to hyperventilate and become dizzy.

"Girl, you okay?" Lez asked, watching Cookie begin to shake while still pointing the gun at Tank lying on the ground.

"I… I never… I never shot anyone before," Cookie spoke with a trembling voice.

Lez walked over to Cookie and pried the gun from her locked grip.

"Well, I'm glad you came thru," Lez started, standing over Tank's body. She nudged his foot with her own to see if he would move.

"This bastard really wanted to do me in," she said to Cookie while pointing her gun at Tank. "Look at ya now, batty boy." She eased in closer to Tank's already dead body and added, "Now you can say wzup to ya brother ya damn self." POW!

"What the fuck was that?" Josh shot out the house in a panic. "Who shooting now?"

He glanced over at Cookie, who was pointing at Lez.

"He ain't dead enough for ya?" Josh joked.

"Y'all gotta go, man; I know the police on the way."

As he finished his statement, they could hear the sirens from afar off getting closer.

"See, yall better dip."

Cookie ran to the car, while Lez walked over to Josh with gun in hand.

"I'm glad you alright," Josh spoke as Lez was an arm's length away. Sirens were even closer. You could see the red and blues highlighting the skies.

"Ya homegirl a rider," Josh stated calmly, as Lez eased her gun upward, inches away from his testicles.

"She is," Lez confirmed. "So when we come back, have the rest of my money."

* * *

CLUB HEAVY'S

"How you looking on your end?" Heavy asked to the person on his phone.

The streets were starting to dry up. It's been hit and miss for the last eight months. Tiger was usually the top provider to the streets, but he has been M.I.A.

Heavy nor Lez has been able to find a steady connect that was on the level to provide as Tiger did.

"Well hit me up if you hear something?" he continued, trying not to express anger.

Club Heavy's made a steady income, however it never brought in the income he received from the streets.

"I need a minimum of fifty to a hunnit bricks if you can find it."

The voice on the other end expressed that they could maybe get three to five kilos. Nowhere near the 50 or 100 kilos Heavy so desperately wanted.

Heavy kept in contact with Tiger, but tiger was still in hiding. Detective Holzendorf has yet to let go of the Operation Tigers Den case. They had to tread lightly.

"Keep me posted" Heavy responded before hanging up.

"FUCK!" he snapped, leaning back in his office chair.

"Boss." He heard a voice say as his office door creep open and one of his security guys enter. "You got two women hear to see you."

"Two women?" Heavy repeated, confused.

"Who is it?'

"They wouldn't say," the guard added quickly. "She just insisted I do my damn job and don't worry 'bout who she is." Heavy smiled, because he knew only one woman who would make an entrance like that.

"Let 'em up."

He sat up in his chair, then stood as his door swung open.

"Leslie Hill," he said with a smile. "Or should I say, Big Lez." He walked over and gave her a hug. "What brings you 'round my parts? If my memory serves me correctly, you told me you would never step foot in my little club, 'cause it was…" He paused. "What's the word you used?" "GHETTO?" she chimed in quickly.

"Yeah, that's the word. GHETTO."

They both smiled and hugged again.

"I'm here 'cause I brought someone with me.

"Oh yeah, my security said it was two of y'all." He clasped his hands together. "What, you brought me a snack?"

"As big as you is, you don't need no more damn snacks," Lez joked.

"Oh, we ranking?" Heavy snapped back, as Lez walked outside the door and fanned for her guest to appear.

Heavy's eyes lit up when Cookie entered his office.

"OOOOOH SHIT!" he said excitedly, trotting over to Cookie and embracing her. "Wzup lil sis?" "Wzup, Heavy," Cookie responded, happy to be one step closer to Tiger. She felt if anyone knew where he was, it would be Heavy. "Come in and have a seat," Heavy said, guiding them deeper into his office.

Cookie glanced around, wondering when Tiger would jump out to surprise her. She had a rough day, and a reunion would be all she needed.

"First and foremost, welcome home," he said to Cookie.

He noticed Cookie looking around his club in wonder, so he asked, "Where are my manners? Can I get y'all something to drank?"

"Water with lemon," Cookie spoke.

"Anything brown," Lez snapped quickly. "Anything brown, huh?" Heavy joked.

"And you call my club ghetto."

"Don't judge me," Lez defended. "We had a hectic day; I need a drank."

"So, what brings y'all round my way?" Heavy asked. But before Lez could get her sentence started, Heavy asked, "Y'all hollered at Tiger yet?"

Cookie became very attentive as Lez answered. "Nah, it's been a minute. Have you?"

"Shiiiiiiiiit," Heavy stated while in deep thought. "Come to think of it, it's been a minute for me too."

Cookie's heart dropped. Her thought of this being a visit to meet up with Tiger was shot with a few words.

"About six or seven months if I recall."

"So, none of y'all talked to Tiger for over seven months?" Cookie jumped in with a panicked voice. "How y'all know he not dead?"

"Sis, he alright," Heavy assured in his calm voice. "Tiger my main man. If he was dead, he woulda told me."

"Boy, you stupid," Lez stated jokingly. Cookie, on the other hand, did not find it funny.

"I see y'all with the jokes today," Cookie began. "Y'all don't know how it was for me. Gone for over three years and not receive ONE letter, ONE visit, not even a Happy Birthday card." She wiped away a tear as she struggled to continue. "It's like I was dead to the world."

Lez wiped the inner part of her eye to stop a tear that was forming.

"In his defense, lil sis," Heavy began, walking over to Cookie to comfort her, "he couldn't make moves like that, 'cause that detective dude was watching and waiting for him to surface."

Cookie gave Heavy a *none of that matters* look "But he always kept ya commissary stacked," Heavy added.

"Bump a damn commissary," she stated angrily. "That's the bare minimum he coulda done, being I was in there cause of him."

(awkward pause)

"Nah, the hell with that!" Cookie snapped. "He could have sent an anonymous letter with no return address, with a picture of a heart in it, or a bird, or just the words I LOVE YOU in it." She sniffed several times, paused to breath then added. "Instead, I Got Nothing."

Cookie, Heavy, and Lez all joined in a group hug. The moment was interrupted when Lez's phone chimed. She noticed it was one of her big customers. Unfortunately, she did not have enough product to fulfill his order. She really wanted to keep this client happy, because he definitely keeps her happy with the money he spends.

"How you looking on work?" Lez asked Heavy as she pulled away from the group hug, staring at her ringing phone.

"I'm looking kinda ugly myself," he responded, then asked, "What you need?"

"About 10 bricks."

"Oooo-wee," Heavy huffed, then walked back to his desk. "I'm probably only sittin' on 'bout 10 bricks myself."

Lez let out a sigh of disappointment as Heavy continued. "Shit's real ugly right now. I can probably give you about three or four."

"Hell, I got three or four myself," Lez chimed in. "I need these for my big customer, but I don't wanna be completely out."

"Shit, I don't wanna be out neither," Heavy added. "Shit ain't been the same since Tiger been in hiding. The streets starving."

"I know, right," Lez joined in. "We better do something, and fast."

Cookie, although she wasn't eavesdropping, overheard Lez and Heavy's conversation, and decided to chime in.

"Are y'all talking 'bout drugs?" Cookie asked in wonder.

Lez and Heavy stared at each other, trying to hold back laughter.

"What's funny?" Cookie asked, being serious.

"I used to hear Tiger say something about some bricks a lot. But I always thought he was talking about bricks for houses or some kind of construction, 'cause he used to get two and three hundred of them."

Both Lez and Heavy nodded in unison, reminiscing on the days they would be flooded with dope supplied by Tiger.

"Girl, what you know 'bout bricks?" Lez asked with a smirk.

"Absolutely nothing!" Cookie snapped back. "But my uncle, well, my auntie's ex-husband Tyrone, I think he a big-time drug dealer."

"How you know that man a drug dealer?"

Heavy asked.

"Cause my auntie only mess with street dudes. And he drives real expensive cars, always fly, and always on trips."

"How you get drug dealer out of that?" Lez added. "He could be an entrepreneur or something."

"Nah!" Cookie began. "I watched Tiger move the exact same way as Tyrone would move, and my auntie used to always have to go pick up money from various places for him also."

"I still don't hear drug dealer out of that,"

Heavy joined back in. "I deposit money every day for the club."

"Well, it's only one way to find out."

Cookie asked Lez for her phone and dialed her Auntie Steph's number.

"Praise the Lord." A very familiar voice answered, bringing a smile to Cookie face.

"Hey Auntie." Cookie said happily.

"Who is this?"

"This ya niece, Cookie."

"Oh, hey baaaby. I haven't heard from you in a long while, how you been?"

"I've been good auntie, how bout yaself." Cookie asked dragging around the question.

"Get to the point." Lez whispered in Cookie ear. *"I'm fine, Suga, Blessed and highly favored."* Steph stated.

"That's good, Auntie," Cookie began. She caught eyes with Lez and lip-synced the words, "O.k., Ima do it."

"Auntie, let me ask you a question."

"What's that, baby?"

"You still talk to Uncle Tyrone?" Cookie felt nervous about her aunt's response.

"Oh no, baby!" Steph began. *"I cut that off years ago, baby."*

"Why? What happened?" Cookie asked, hoping she would reveal he is a drug dealer.

"We just went down two different paths, puddin'. I went with the Lord, and he went with the streets."

"What you mean, Auntie? Was he a drug dealer or something?"

Lez nodded with the questions Cookie was asking as Heavy sat back listening.

"He was definitely something, baby. He did some of everything. It was way too much for me to continue to be a part of."

"You wouldn't happen to still have his number, would you?"

"And if I did, why would you want it?" Steph asked feeling Cookie was being suspicious.

"No biggie, just wanna catch up."

"Don't lie to me, lil Girl." Auntie Steph snapped. *"I don't know what your purpose is for looking for Tyrone, but I'm telling you to not do it. He a bad man."*

"I just wanna catch up, that's all." Cookie lied. *"You were always a terrible liar."*

Outside of Aunt Steph's long lecture and pleading, she ended up giving Cookie Tyrone's number.

"Okay now, you been warned," Steph added. "Thanx, Auntie," Cookie stated with a smile. "I'ma come sit with ya sometime next week." *"You just flowing out lies, aren't ya."* Steph joked.

Before Cookie and Steph hung up Steph stated, *"Tell Tyrone I asked about him."*

Cookie took the paper she wrote Tyrone's number on and flashed it in front of Heavy and Lez.

"Now is the moment of truth," she stated as she began to dial.

When she dialed the last digit, she heard the phone ring once and hung up immediately.

"Why you hung up? What happened?" Lez pondered excitedly.

"What if it's the wrong number!" Cookie continued. "What if he don't remember me! What if he married, and his wife answers?""What if you call and find out. How 'bout that," Lez joked.

"I don't know what to say." She began, then looked over at Heavy and asked, "What do you think I should say?"

"You know what I think?" Heavy chimed in. Cookie sat in wonder as Heavy stated, "I think you need ta caaaaall Tyrooooone."

"Caaaaall him," Lez added in joke.

Before Cookie could decide to make the call, Lez's phone rang. It was the number Cookie had just called. Cookie extended the phone out to Lez to answer, being it was her phone. But Lez ushered the phone back to Cookie, urging her to answer it.

"Hello," Cookie whispered into the phone. *"Did someone just call this number?"* a deep male voice asked. Lez and heavy was confident it was him.

"Yes." She stated nervously. "I was looking for a mister Tyrone."

"This is he. Who dis?"

There was a nervous pause. Lez and Heavy were excited. Now they just gotta prove that he could help them how they need help. Cookie cleared her throat then continued.

"This Sar—" she caught herself mid-introduction. "This Cookie."

"I'm not sure I know anyone name Cookie." *"I'm not sure I know anyone name Cookie."*

It had been over 10 years since she seen or talked to this man. She felt stupid for even calling him now, but she had to see it thru. She had come too far to turn back now.

"You used to date my Auntie Steph," Cookie stated with confidence.

"STEPH!" he responded excitedly.

"This lil Cookie?"

Lez, Heavy and Cookie all smiled.

"How you been, darling?"

41

"Good." She stated bluntly.

"How is Steph?"

"She good. She told me to tell you hey."

"That was my baby."

There was a brief pause before Tyrone asked.*"What do I owe the privilege of this call?"*

"I need to talk to you about something." Cookie stated in her low-toned voice.

"Okay, what's up." Tyrone asked curiously.

"I can't talk about it over the phone."

"Is everything okay?" he asked confused.

"It is. But it's about business."

"Business? what kind of business?"

She looked around at Lez and Heavy for help, she didn't wanna say anything incriminating on the phone.

"Say construction." Heavy chimed in.

Cookie had a confused look on her face, but he reiterated the construction comment.

"Trust Me."

"Construction business," Cookie spoke.

"What type of business, you said?" Tyrone asked confused.

Heavy wrote a statement on a piece of paper and handed it to Cookie to read over the phone. "You want me to say this?" she asked removing the phone from her face.

"Just read it."

Cookie paused for a moment, then read the paper like a teleprompter.

"I'm teamed up with some people in the construction business and I'm-"

She again paused, feeling awkward about the words about to come from her mouth.

"Say the words."

Heavy gritted thru his teeth.

"I'm teamed up with some people in the construction business, and we short on a steady supply of bricks."

"Bricks?" Tyrone repeated confused.

"Yes. Bricks," Cookie confirmed staring at Lez and Heavy.

"This ain't the right dude." Lez assumed.

"He has no idea what you talking about.

Before Cookie could try to repair whatever mistake she had just started, Tyrone blurted out, *"Ooooohh Briiiiiiiicks."*

Cookie's eyes widened. Could this be real? Was she setting up a drug deal? This day had started and ended crazy.

Tyrone gave Cookie another number to contact him on to further talk about the construction business. They also planned to meet face to face to hash out all the details on how Tyrone handles his business-prices, quantity, etc.

This was it. Lez and Heavy were about to be back on top. But with all the happiness going on within the room, Cookie only thought about one thing. Tiger.

Did he know she was out?

And most importantly... did he even care?

5

Blood & Ice

Several weeks had passed, and everything was back right with the streets. The weather was snowing with cocaine again, and the money was raining in the city once more. Everyone was happy. Well, almost everyone. And everyone was eating; well, almost everyone. Again.

Lez and Heavy were on top of their game and making a lot more money under Cookie's connect than they ever did under Tiger's connect.

But Lez noticed that even though more money was being made, Cookie stayed regular. She wore the same rotation of clothing she had before the connection was made and was still living in one of her guest rooms. Lez didn't mind though; she enjoyed the company. She didn't trust many women because they would always end up in some type of woman-jealousy spat because she refused to date a specific guy. Or if the girl had a boyfriend, he would end up liking Lez, and the girl would falsely accuse Lez of plotting to sleep with their man.

Lez found it a lot easier to be solo, and if she did find a guy who was worthy to give herself to for an intimate game of Bust and Go, no real name or real numbers were exchanged.

It was a semi-lonely life. Being that she couldn't find a worthy man to marry, she decided to marry the game. It treats her good, and it helped her put a ring on it.

Lez had come home one day from shopping. She had bought her and

Cookie outfits and designer bags. Lez decided her and Cookie would make a guest appearance to Club Heavy's. With the upgrade in product quantity and the unexpected price drop, Heavy decided to have a special gathering for the ladies, with special invited guests.

Lez walked in Cookie's room. She didn't see her, but she could hear the shower running. She dropped the bags she bought for Cookie on the bed and slowly crept toward the bathroom. The door was slightly cracked, and Lez could swear she could hear moaning.

I know this bitch don't have a nigga in my house, she thought as she crept to the door. Lez looked in on Cookie and smiled with delight.

"Okay girl, I see ya," Lez mumbled to herself, watching Cookie masturbate with the help of Lez's massage pulse showerhead.

After several intense minutes of watching, Lez couldn't take it anymore. She began undressing herself, rubbed on her throbbing womanhood, and quietly walked in the bathroom. She eased closer and continued watching as the water beaded down on Cookie's body. Standing within arm's reach, Lez stared for an additional moment. She then eased her hand down and touched Cookie's breast, which startled her dramatically.

"What the hell are you doing?" she asked angrily, yet embarrassed. Lez remained silent.

Cookie stood up and clasped her arms over her breasts. Lez gently tried to remove her arms from being folded. Cookie resisted at first, repeating "What are you doing" during every touch, but Lez was persistent, and Cookie was succumbing to Lez's enchantment.

They both stood inches from each other, bodies glistening from the steamy shower.

In prison, Cookie may have felt this was wrong, but today it felt completely right. The way Lez caressed her breast, massaged and sucked on her nipples, the way she gently yet dominantly sucked on her tongue when she kissed her. She loved the way Lez took control, tugging her, pushing her, bending her over; it's as if she was hearing her inner thoughts. Cookie gripped Lez's head firmly when her tongue rotated around her clit. The sensation of the shower water with the magic of Lez's tongue was way more than Cookie could handle.

Maybe it was being locked up for years and not being touched by someone other than herself; but she could feel her soul escaping her body when she climaxed. She'd had several intense orgasms with Tiger, but this was way more intense. She had heard of a woman squirting, but she didn't think she was capable of accomplishing such a task. It was so many moving parts; Cookie couldn't keep up. Her eyes rolled back, her whole body trembled, she tried to brace on anything she could find, and with a loud scream, she squirted everywhere.

Lez stood up with a bright smile, and a face full of Cookie's orgasm. Cookie felt embarrassed; this had never happened to her before. Although everything about the encounter felt right—the squirting, and the being with a woman—Lez stood inches away from Cookie's face with a bright Kool-Aid smile.

"I'm sorry," Cookie stated, blushed. "This has never—"

Before she could finish her sentence, Lez dove in and tongue-kissed Cookie passionately, allowing her to taste her own essence.

They both took a moment in the shower, allowing the water to wash this moment down the drain.

* * *

"You still with that guy you were with when I was with your aunt?" Tyrone asked, as he was meeting Cookie for their normal shipment pickup meeting at Waffle House.

"His name is Tiger," Cookie snapped at Tyrone's question. "And yes, we are still together."

"Cool," Tyrone nodded.

"Weeeell," Cookie spoke, seeming depressed. Tyrone noticed her head drop and the mood change.

"What is it?" Tyrone asked, taking a sip of his coffee.

"It's just—" She hesitated a moment, contemplating should she have this conversation with this man.

46

On one hand, he dated her aunt when she was young, and now he supplies her man's friends with drugs. But on the other hand, she don't really know him.

"It's what!" he asked, curious like a parent. "Come on now. You can talk to me."

"Can I!" she snapped with a serious look. "Cause my aunt say she loved you a lot, but you a bad man for real, for real."

Tyrone sat up in his chair and adjusted his shirt as he took everything in Cookie just laid on him. He knew the life he lived, but he never heard it being bestowed on him the way Cookie was giving it to him.

He always wondered why Steph just changed suddenly. Had his way of life scared her that much? This is her niece. If things ever went south or money get messed up, could he spare her for the sake of Steph?

Cookie never knew Tiger used to deal with Tyrone. She also didn't know they are beefing over the hit Tyrone put on his brother, and that Tiger killing Tyrone's henchman years ago.

"You know what, Mr. Tyrone," Cookie began. "I don't know if I'm cut out for this. I'm doing this for some of my boyfriend friends. I'm not benefiting financially from this AT ALL. I just recently got out of jail for some similar shit like this, and I don't plan on going back. And to make matters worse, I think my boyfriend has moved on, and I took a charge to keep him out of jail.""WOW!" Tyrone responded, hearing Cookie's testimony.

He spent the next two hours helping Cookie understand the dope game— how to make profit, weigh dope, and traffic product. He coached her the same way he coached Steph before she decided enough was enough. When Cookie left Tyrone, she had a new outlook on how she would approach the game.

She decided that if she was gonna be in it, she may as well master it to be the best at it. She felt the day Tiger see her again would be the day she would be looked upon as a Queen of the Game."Alright, Mr. Tyrone. I think I got enough information to get me started."

Tyrone nodded in agreement with a proud smile on his face as Cookie continued.

"It's time for me to say goodbye to Cookie, and introduce the world to Lady C."

"That's what's up," Tyrone spoke proudly.

"And from now on, you no longer need to call me Tyrone. You can call me by what my business partners know me as."

"And what's that?" Cookie asked.

Tyrone stood up from the table, left money for the bill and a large tip, and replied,

"ICE."

* * *

A few months had passed, and Cookie was starting to make a name for herself. Lez was no longer the only diamond shining in Duval County.

Cookie had saved up enough to get her a nice crib in Marsh Landing. It wasn't as exquisite as Lez's place, but she hadn't been in the game as long as Lez neither.

She upgraded her wardrobe, got some jewelry, and bought herself the all-white Audi R8 V10. Life was good. Every day it seemed Tiger would get farther and farther from her mind.

"Girl, let's go out tonight?" Cookie asked Lez while they were at the nail shop.

Lez glanced over at Cookie, who was hopping around in her seat excitedly.

"Girl, you starting to like to be outside a hell of a lot."

"It's boring being cooped up in that house all the time by myself," Cookie snapped back.

"Then get you a butler and some maids and you won't be," Lez began, pointing at a chipped part of her nail she wanted fixed.

Cookie smirked, but Lez could tell the money and the life was grabbing her fast.

"The worst thing you wanna do," Lez started, glancing over at Cookie, "is to be too accessible in these streets. You wanna keep a certain level of wonder about yourself."

Cookie paused. She respected Lez because she has been the talk of the city for years. She oozed respect. Plus, when she was with Tiger, she was a lady—very exclusive, mysterious, but a homebody. This new level of power had her feeling herself.

"We are hood celebrities to some people, and to keep that status, you can't just be mingling with the common folk. Everything must be VIP. We don't stand in lines, we don't wait for tables, we don't even go to certain block parties."

Cookie's eyes widened, because those are the things she enjoyed with Tiger. "We are exclusive backstage bitches now!"

Cookie stayed quiet as Lez broke down the laws of being a Boss Bitch. It was a lot to take in. When Lez was done, she quoted the phrase, *With great power comes great responsibility.*

* * *

Focusing on the future and how far they could get, Cookie and Lez never anticipated their recent past would surface sooner than later. The murder in Picketville was still unsolved, and the police were not giving up on the investigation. The story Josh had given the police panned out to be a dead end; a made-up story. So, they watched him until he slipped up, and slipped up he did.

He was brought in for doing a hand-to-hand drug deal to a confidential informant—7 grams of cocaine and 7 grams of fentanyl.

That small amount could cost him years in jail and tens of thousands of dollars to fight in court. He didn't have the time or the money; so, he decided to cooperate with the cops.

Fortunately, he only knew Leslie as Big Lez, and he never got Cookie's name, but he was very good at his descriptive image of them both.

They confiscated his phone, trying to use the number he called Lez from. But Lez is always eight steps ahead. She uses a burner phone and changes numbers frequently. All he knew for certain was that Lez was a part of Ken Knight Mafia and the Swiss Cheese Gang.

Detective Holzendorf was called in for this one, being that it was a part of his still-active case, Operation Tiger's Den. The detective was still angry, being that he never got Tiger, and those he was gonna indict were either found dead or there wasn't enough evidence to convict. He did get one conviction, he thought, glancing over the mugshot of Cookie. He always felt her to be a casualty of war, hoping her conviction would lure Tiger out of hiding.

It was very strange to the detective, though, that it was two girls involved, and the unknown girl fit the description of Cookie almost to a tee.

He leaned back in his office chair with his hands clasped to the back of his head and thought, *What would be the odds that this is the same girl we had in custody, and she got away with just a minor conspiracy... to find out she really had a major involvement in my case after all.*

He sat up, made a printed copy of Cookie's mugshot, stared at it, and mumbled, "And you betta pray I don't find out you may also be involved in this murder."

Detective Holzendorf met up with Josh to show him a picture of Cookie. He confirmed that was her, and he also implicated her as the shooter.

This was getting more and more interesting to Holzendorf. If he couldn't get Tiger before, he felt he now had a way to tear down the whole house from inside out. He sat in his car pondering at the picture once again and said, "Okay young lady, you wanna play big boy games, well prepare to win big boy prizes."

* * *

Heavy was throwing his yearly Celebration of Life remembrance party for his homeboy PieYay, who was killed by Six, one of Ice's henchmen.

Lez and Cookie pulled up at the front entrance in Cookie's new Audi R8. Valet took her keys, and Heavy had security meet them outside to escort them to Tiger's VIP area. He sent up a bottle of Tiger's favorite champagne, and since Lez liked brown, he sent her a special bottle of Louis XIII.

He nodded and smiled from his office window when they looked up to thank him. The crowd was live, and the vibe was right. Heavy had a special guest appearance from Trick Daddy and JT Money, being they were PieYay's favorite artists.

Lez and Cookie were enjoying themselves, dancing and mingling with the common folk; so much so, that they caught the attention of two young gentlemen who felt they would shoot their shot.

One of the guys walked up on Lez, smiled, and began to dance. He was cute, she thought—respectable and could move, so she eased closer to let him know she was feeling him also. Cookie, on the other hand, the guy that stepped to her had one too many drinks and was very handsy and aggressive.

She tried to be nice at first by politely moving him away and stepping aside without missing a beat. Lez noticed the encounter, but felt it was handled peacefully.

Unfortunately, the guy did not get the hint; he continued to tug on Cookie despite her reactions.
"Listen here, dude,"
Cookie snapped as she stopped dancing.
"I don't wanna dance with you. I'm good."
She attempted to walk away and move closer to Lez and her friend where it seemed safe."BITCH!" he blurted, tugging her arm. "Do you know who I am?"
"BIIIIITCH!"
she snapped back and turned to face him. "I GOT YOUR BITCH, PUSSY NIGGA!"
Lez walked up and tried to deescalate the situation calmly. She felt she was too fly to be fighting tonight.
"Listen here, my guy," she spoke softly but stern. "She say she don't wanna dance, so keep it pushing. It's a lot more easier girls in here, go get them."

They attempted to walk through the crowd back to their area when the guy blurted:
"Fuck that bitch. I ain't want her anyway." "NOBODY AIN'T WANT YOUR DIRTY ASS NEITHER!" Cookie spazzed, screaming over Lez's shoulder.

A nearby guy was lightly holding Cookie back as she was trying to get to the disrespectful guy. Lez, being free, walked over to him and stated,

"Call her a bitch again."

The guy leaned in closer and stated,

"What you gonna do, huh?"

The look on Lez's face became intense as the guy added, "I should rob y'all ass."

He noticed the diamond necklace and bracelets both Cookie and Lez were wearing. He could barely stand, he was so intoxicated.

Lez could see security rummaging their way through the crowd to get to them.

"These bitches don't know who the fuck I am," the guy slurred to a guy witnessing the encounter.

"This the Boujie Bitch Bunch," he added.

When he tried to turn back to face Lez, she quickly grabbed the four-thousand-dollar bottle of Louis Heavy gave them and slammed it across the head of the guy—knocking him unconscious almost immediately.

When security finally made it through the crowd, Lez grabbed their purses and was preparing to leave. Heavy met them downstairs by the door to apologize.

"I told you your shit was ghetto," Lez exclaimed, getting into the passenger seat of Cookie's car.

Cookie embraced Heavy, when over his shoulder in the crowd she noticed a guy wearing a casual denim outfit, white tee, large Cuban link diamond chain with matching bracelet, and all-white Forces. He looked very familiar. She started the car, rolled down her window, and eased by to get a better look.

They caught eyes. His facial expression confirmed her suspicion. Her heart dropped, and blood boiled. As she drove by, he stepped out of line and into the road watching them ride into the night.

"You know him?" Lez asked, noticing Cookie adjusting her rearview angrily.

"Yeah, I know that bastard," Cookie confirmed, still looking in her rearview making sure they weren't being tailed. "He the reason I'm in this shit I'm in."

"Who is he?" Lez asked.

Cookie turned her attention toward Lez and stated, "His name Detective

Holzendorf."

6

Crown of Lies

Detective Holzendorf was getting tired of trying to find the two women involved in the Picketville murder. He felt he had a strong lead with Serena Loveless (Cookie) being the prime suspect.

He tried the address she had on file that she said she would be staying at after her release, but that was a dead-end address.

He decided if he couldn't get to her, he would make her come to him. He decided to link the information he had on her to the Channel 9 news. Someone would turn her in if they felt a reward was involved.

If she thinks she's innocent, then she'll show up. If not, she'll stay on the run, and then the city and the system will deem her guilty anyway. *He was done playing her game*, he thought to himself.

* * *

Cookie pulled up to her residence bewildered and fatigued. She wanted a hot shower, a hot meal, and a long nap before she meets up with Ice later that evening.

As she was getting out of her car, about to grab the duffel bag full of money, she was startled.

"Hey neighbor."

"OH, MY JESUS!" she blurted out in fear. She turned quickly to see her nosey neighbor, Mrs. Baker. "You can't be creeping up on people like that, Mrs. Baker."

Mrs. Baker was a 65-year-old mixed lady, who doesn't look a day older than 45, from professional lipo. She has beautiful curly silver hair, and a 20-year-old's breast and butt. She was widowed four years ago when her husband died from a heart attack while they were having sex.

Her husband left her a large sum of money in a life insurance policy, so now Mrs. Baker hires young men to occasionally come by and work her out. "Some man came by here looking for you," Mrs. Baker stated, trying to look around Cookie to see if someone was in the car with her.

"What man!" Cookie interjected.

"Some handsome-looking young man," Mrs. Baker began to describe. "He was tall, well dressed, nice build, pecan-tan complexion, nice butt."

"That's not helping, Mrs. Baker," Cookie joked. "Well, he looked to be between 30 to 35 years old."

Cookie still didn't know anyone to fit that description until Mrs. Baker said, "He coulda been some type of officer or something."

"How do you know that?" Cookie wondered, now paying attention.

"Because I could see a badge and a gun on his hip."

"Why you didn't start with that, Mrs. Baker!" Cookie snapped, worried.

Who was this cop that came by trying to find her, and what did he want? What she was doing wasn't quite legal. But from what she knows about police raids, they're not going to come and knock on your door looking for you. They are going to kick in your door when you least expect it.

After Cookie and Mrs. Baker talked for a few more minutes, Cookie went in the house, threw the money on the bed, and was about to take a long hot bath when she noticed a mugshot of her flash across the TV screen.

"What the hell is going on here," she mumbled, turning the volume up. Kimberly Longview was reporting.

"I'm standing on the corner of Moncrief and Spicer where just a few months ago, Rashod Williams, known to his friends and family as Tank, was gunned down over what law enforcement are looking into as a lovers' spat."

Cookie watched as they placed a picture of the guy she shot when Lez was in trouble. She was also wondering why her picture popped up first, and what for.

Her question was answered when the reporter Kimberly continued:

"This is the woman in question in regard to the case that police are looking for."

They plastered a picture of Cookie's mugshot on the screen. In the picture, she looked high, her hair was blown everywhere, she looked like she needed to be in a drug rehab facility.

"What in the—" Cookie couldn't finish the sentence. She was in such dismay that she couldn't fathom her next thoughts.

The reporter went on to say that if anyone knew the whereabouts of—and they plastered Cookie's real name (Serena Loveless) across the screen—to contact Crime Stoppers.

"This is bad! This is bad! This is bad!" she repeated, pacing around in circles.

That would explain the cop coming to her house, she thought. She was afraid to shower and nap as she previously planned. She felt that an officer would circle back, see her car, then forcefully enter as they always do in situations like this.

She didn't have many places to go. But she remembered she still had Lez's house key. She cleared out all the money she had for her and Ice, packed it in her car, and drove to Queen's Harbor.

* * *

JSO interrogation Room

"I'ma need you to wire up and reach out to Big Lez and her accomplice that was with her the night Rashod Williams was killed," Detective Holzendorf stated, prepping Josh on what he needed from him to bring Lez and Cookie to justice.

"Man, I can't do that," Josh pleaded with a saddened look on his face. "It's bad enough I told you what I already did. But I can't wire up."

Det. Holzendorf stood up out his chair as Josh continued.

"Don't you have enough to make an arrest? Hell, I identified them and told you how to find them. What more do you want?"

"You think the little shit you gave me so far is an even swap for the shit I got on you?" the detective threatened. "You are looking at hard time if I was to submit the charges I got on you."

"What charges?" Josh snapped. "I may be looking at two years. Tops." Holzendorf sat on the edge of his desk facing Josh and crossed his arms. "I just felt like, I scratch your back, you scratch mine," Josh added.

"Two years! Is this what you think you will get?" Holzendorf started. "When I'm done with my report, you may be lucky to get ten years."

"Man, it was just 7 grams of coke and 7 grams of Fetty," Josh reminded.

"That's not what I remember," the detective spoke. "If I recall, we may have confiscated 18 ounces of coke and 9 ounces of fentanyl."

"But that's not the truth, and you know it," Josh snapped angrily.

"You think the judge gonna care about the truth?" Holzendorf smirked. "I'm a highly decorated detective, and to them you are a common everyday thug. Putting you away would be his privilege."

Josh sat quietly and nervously as Det. Holzendorf continued to discuss with him all the things he needed from him to make this plan work.

"Look at it like this," Holzendorf spoke as they were about done. "My motto has always been: why do ten when you can send a friend."

* * *

"How are you this evening, madam?" Timothy, Big Lez's butler, spoke as Cookie walked into Lez's house.

"I'm good, Tim!" Cookie responded, looking around the house, about to go to the guest room she had been using when staying with Lez.

"Ms. Hill isn't in at the moment. Can I get you anything?" Timothy asked.

"Nah, I'm good," Cookie started. "I'ma just run upstairs, take a shower, get a lil rest, then I'll show myself out."

"I'll alert Ms. Hill!" Timothy responded with a nod as he was about to walk off.

"No, don't disturb her," Cookie interjected. "I'll call her myself in a bit."

Cookie sat in the shower for an extended period of time. She pondered the situation she'd seen previously about herself on the news.

How would this play out? What could she say? Who was the guy that came by her house?

Her head was spinning a mile a minute. Where was Tiger when she needed him? He has never not been there for her when things looked as impossible as they do now.

She decided to lie down and rest. Her mind and body needed a reset.

"Can I get you anything?" Tim the butler asked right at the nick of time.

"Yes," Cookie spoke quickly. "Can I get two Excedrin, a bottled water—" she paused, then uttered the words, "—and the number to a good lawyer."

Cookie woke up a few hours later, body refreshed, mind clear and ready to face the world and its many obstacles. She looked at her phone; she had several missed calls from Ice, and a couple from Heavy. He needed to re-up, and she knew Ice just wanted his money. She'll call them back, she thought.

She stepped outside into the hallway. It was quiet. No Timothy, no staff, and no Lez.

She headed toward Lez's room, assuming she may be home but just resting. She knocked twice, then slowly opened the door, saying Lez's name every foot the door opened.

The room was clear. Cookie noticed there was another door in Lez's room that was not the closet nor the bathroom. The light was on, so she went to explore... Lez may be inside.

The room was beautiful. There was a mural of twin baby angels painted on the wall. In the middle of the floor was a clear glass case on a pedestal, with a letter inside titled *Letters to My Angels*.

"I didn't know Lez was ever pregnant," Cookie mumbled, as she was drawn in to read the letter.

I would like to first apologize for not getting the chance to ever meet you all. I lost you before I even knew you. The way you were taken from me, I often wonder was that God's will.

Did he feel I wouldn't be able to handle motherhood? If so, then why choose me in the first place...

Your mother has done a lot of bad things, and I've taken several sons and daughters from their parents; so maybe God decided I needed to know how it feels to have my kids taken from me and be forced to live with it.

Cookie's eyes watered as she read Lez's heartwarming letter.

I never got the chance to hold you, or feel you grow inside me, but it feels like my soul has been ripped away. I hope at Judgement Day God allow me to at least speak to you before he cast me away.

Y'all would have loved your life; your parents are the best to ever do it. Although your dad never knew you existed, I'm sure he would love y'all also. Y'all will be forever missed.

Cookie had a different type of respect and sympathy for Lez at this point. She saw her in a new light. She was a person capable of loving someone other than herself. And with the hospitality she was shown by Lez, Cookie could see her as a real friend. Or so she thought. Her tone changed when she read the last lines of the letter.

Love Mommy and Dad,

Leslie Hill & Antonio McMillan

"ANTONIO McMillan?" Cookie snapped. Was Lez insinuating Tiger was the alleged father of her deceased kids?

The tears she once had in her eyes for the sympathy for Lez were now tears of anger and vengeance.

"This bitch been key keying in my face, knowing this whole time she been fucking my man."

Cookie's mind was all disoriented at this point. This could not go unanswered. She looked for a way to remove the letter from inside the glass container. The thought crossed her mind to just break the glass, but what would that accomplish? She was angry and befuddled, but she wasn't a heartless animal. She took a picture of the letter in the case and walked out.

While Cookie was gathering her things, Heavy called her once again. She was considering ignoring the call, but remembered this was Tiger's Ace in the hole. Surely, he would know if Tiger and Lez were indeed sleeping together and had babies on the way.

The letter was clear, but Cookie wanted to know who all were involved in this horrific scandal.

"Yeah," she answered in a dry voice.

"Wzup lil sis," Heavy started, relieved to hear her answer. "You ain't forgot about me, have you?" "Nah," she stated, trying not to lash out. "Just a lot going on right now."

"I can imagine," he snapped back. "I saw ya picture on the news. Are you good?"

"I don't know at this point," she added, sounding defeated.

"You miss bruh, huh?" Heavy chimed in, trying to lighten the conversation.

Normally Cookie would jump to respond to that question, but finding her new information, her reason for wanting to see Tiger transformed from hugs and kisses to punches and kicks. She felt lost, betrayed, and even more, alone. The three and a half years she done to prove her loyalty felt in vain at this point.

"Was I used just to get me out the picture? Is that why he has been ignoring me, because he felt guilty about the pregnancy?" Cookie thought, as she responded to Heavy.

"Let me ask you a question," she began. "And I need you to be VERY honest."

"Oh shit," Heavy panicked. "What happened?""Nothing yet."

As she was about to ask Heavy all the questions she needed answered, she received another call. It was Ice. She had been so busy that she forgot she had to meet him to drop off the money and get the new pick-up spot.

The way she was feeling, she didn't know if she even wanted to do this anymore. Everything had been a lie. The money, the life, Lez's friendship toward her... even Tiger.

"I gotta call ya back, Heavy," Cookie started. "It's the plug."

"Oh, okay," Heavy stated, then added, "Just swing by the club when you get a chance. And bring me 20 outfits."

That was Heavy's code for kilos of cocaine."Alright. See ya in a bit," Cookie ended, then clicked over to speak with Ice.

Cookie met up with Ice. He could tell something was off with her. He quizzed her until she gave in and told him what was going on.

He told her to confront everyone involved, search for the truth. Don't let this go unanswered. Play it smart—this was chess, not checkers.

Cookie decided that's what she would do. Nobody was gonna just play in her face like that. She could never get the time back she spent in jail for the man she felt loved her without limits.

This whole time she felt she was the queen who sacrificed herself to save her king from being checked, just to find out the whole time she was just a pawn.

7

Ride or Die

"I had her ass in my eyesight, and I let her get away," Detective Holzendorf was explaining to one of his colleagues.

"You say you watched them drive off. Did you at least get the tag number?"

"It all happened so fast," Holzendorf stated, sounding disappointed. "Plus, it was dark. I couldn't make it out if I tried."

"And you sure it was her?" Officer Randolph asked. "You did say it was dark."

"I know it was her," Holzendorf snapped, trying to convince the officer. "She was driving a white Audi R8, and she had another girl in the car with her."

"The Audi R8!" Officer Randolph said, surprised. "That car cost over a hunnit grand. Now I ask again, are you sure that was her?"

"Man, I'm telling you, that was her." He was fumbling through some files he had on the Picketville murder and stated, "And those two together fit the description perfectly that we got from that lil knucklehead from round the way." "Well, it seems you have some detective work to do," Randolph responded as he stood up and headed out Holzendorf's office. "I'm 'bout to call it a night."

Holzendorf nodded and began pulling up information on his laptop.

He began playing back the previous night in his mind. He could see clearly it was Sarina Loveless (Cookie).

"Who are you, really?" he mumbled, glancing at Cookie's picture.

He looked at his watch. It was late. He felt he too would call it a night. He clicked off his desk lamp, and before he turned off his computer he stated, "You keep slipping away, but we will meet again, and you can bet ya ass on that."

* * *

"Tiger ain't try to contact none of y'all yet?" Cookie asked Lez while she was dropping off 20 kilos. Lez handed her the duffel bag with the money in it. "Tiger never really called me much anyway," Lez lied. "He would contact Heavy or PieYay when it was about business. They kept me on a need-to-know basis."

"Well hell," Cookie cut in. "I need to know if anyone talked to Tiger."

"Try Heavy!" Lez responded, pulling out one of the kilos. She placed on her latex gloves and surgical mask, preparing to cook up some dope when she added, "I feel that's gonna be your best route."

Cookie left Lez's spot in Washington Heights with the intention of heading home. Her plan was to gather all the cash she received from Heavy and Lez, deduct her cut, then report the rest to Ice as she does every couple of weeks.

She was not aware that when she left Lez's spot, she was being followed. It was early a.m. Not many cars on the road, so there was no sense of urgency to dodge traffic or police traps. She felt life was good. She understood now how Tiger flossed the cars, gifts, and trips like he did on a regular; the money seemed limitless, and she was only supplying Heavy and Lez.

At that moment she wished Tiger was there to see her. Not necessarily in the drug game, but her overall transition. The name Lady C was becoming a neighborhood name.

New Female Queen Pin.

She joked that she would eventually have to get her some security, being she was becoming a hood celebrity.

She never realized that if there's four people watching you: two may be rooting for you, one plotting and waiting on your downfall, and one wants your spot and all you have.

Sitting at the light on the corner of Edgewood and Moncrief. The area was quiet. Cookie was still a bit fatigued from the night prior, so she felt a vacation to somewhere tropical was in order.

The numbers on the *Do Not Walk* indicator on the sidewalk showed it would be 30 more seconds before the light would change.

Her phone lit up in her purse. She reached over in the passenger seat, opened it, and pulled out her phone. When she sat up, about to say hello to the unknown person on the other end, she noticed an armed, masked assailant at her window. She froze, dropped the phone from her ear onto the floor, and slowly kept her hands in clear view.

"Open the door, bitch, or I'ma wet this mutha fucka up!" she heard the voice say through the glass.

Her body froze. She feared getting shot. As she was about to unlock the door, she noticed the light turn green. She hesitated momentarily, pondering a possible escape. The robber assumed her thoughts were on speeding off, so he warned:

"As soon as you try to pull off, I'ma light you up."Cookie's heart pounded frantically as he added, "Now open the fucking door. *NOW!*"

She unlocked the door, and the gunman opened it swiftly and placed the gun barrel to the side of her face.

"Get the fuck out!" he stated softly but firmly. Cookie obeyed, not trying to look at the facial area of the gunman, who was still aiming the gun at her face.

"Back the hell away!" he demanded as he climbed in the passenger seat. The gunman rolled down the window and shut the door.

"Can I at least get my purse?" Cookie asked, teary-eyed.

He glanced over in the passenger seat. Her purse was open; he could see some loose bills and a few credit cards. He put the car in gear and blurted out, "This my purse now, BITCH!" then sped off.

Cookie patted her pockets, hoping she still had her phone, then she remembered, she dropped it on the floor. She had the Find My Phone app but was nowhere near another phone or computer.

She was within a 20-minute walk back to Lez's spot, so she decided to go there. She knew she had to call the police to report the car stolen, and Lez probably had a burner phone to make the call on. Plus, the car came with a tracking system, so retrieving the vehicle wouldn't be a problem.

While she was walking, she realized having security or someone to drive her around is a must.

The sun was starting to light up the sky, and cars began to fill the streets. She could only imagine what the gunman was doing with her car. As she got near Lez's apt, she was relieved the 20 kilos were not still in the car, but panic came over her when she also realized the duffel bag with 200-thousand dollars in it was in the back seat.

"Ice gonna kill me," she mumbled, walking up to Lez's apt.

"What you doing back here?" Lez asked, opening the door looking like a surgical nurse. "And where is your car?"

"I JUST GOT ROBBED!" Cookie responded in a panic.

"ROBBED!" Lez snapped back, taking the beaker off the stove, whipped the content inside with her whisk, then placed it on the table to harden. "ROBBED WHERE? BY WHO?"

"I was at the light on Edgewood and Moncrief, and some guy with a mask ran up on me with a gun and made me get out my car." Cookie sat down at the table trying to gain her composure.

Lez was pissed and wanted vengeance.

"I told you, you can't be driving that damn car around here," Lez scolded. "These niggas vultures, ready to pounce when they think a bitch ain't looking."

"I need to use ya phone," Cookie asked.

"It's on the sofa," Lez responded, placing one of the crack cookies on the table, preparing to cut them into slabs.

"I need to call the police and make a report." "WHOA! WHOA! WHOA!" Lez hurried to Cookie. "You can't send the police round here. These niggas will trip."

"I gotta make a report. How else Ima get my car back?" Cookie stood up, about to head outside to make the call to the police.

"Girl, them type cars come with the GPS tracker," Lez pleaded. "Call the hotline number or something."

"Listen, Lez," Cookie snapped, getting frustrated. "My phone, and any piece of information I have on the car, is in the car."

Lez thought for a moment, looking for any reason to get Cookie to NOT call the police to her spot. Nothing Cookie said convinced her the cops were the way to go until Cookie added: "Plus, the money you not too long ago gave me is in the back seat. And I gotta meet the connect this afternoon."

"Oh hell, bitch, call whoever you need to. Call Obama if you got to. He found Bin Laden—I know he can find ya car, and hopefully the money still in it."

Cookie was about to dial the numbers to contact the police when Lez's phone rang. Cookie paused, then attempted to hand Lez the phone.

"I got all this shit on," she pleaded. "You answer it."

"Hello," Cookie spoke softly.

"Is Cookie there?" the voice asked on the other end.

"This is she," she responded, confused.

"Who is that?" Lez lip-synced to Cookie, wondering who the hell Cookie gave her burner phone number to.

Cookie listened to the voice on the other end in disbelief. The voice stated he got her car back and to come downstairs.

Lez noticed Cookie's puzzled look.

"What he say?" she wondered.

Cookie sat stunned for a moment as the person on the other end hung up the phone. Cookie slowly lowered the phone from her face and caught eyes with Lez.

"What the hell did he say, girl?" Lez repeated curiously.

"He say my car downstairs, and to come get the keys."

"Chic, I know you lying," Lez blurted as she trotted to the window.

"What the helly!" Lez responded, surprised. "Bitch, your car outside."

Cookie ran to the window to confirm her car was in fact outside. She was in such amazement she couldn't speak.

"Did your car drive itself to my damn house?" Lez asked, not seeing no one in or around the car. "How much you paid for this damn car!" she continued, opening the door and stepping out back to survey the area for safety, making sure it wasn't a set up.

"This some Knight Ryder type shit," she added as they both crept downstairs, noticing the engine was still running.

As they crept even closer to the car, about to open the door, a deep voice said, "You welcome."

Lez turned quickly toward the voice with her arms extended out, hands clasped together, mimicking as if she was holding a gun.

Cookie saw the guy come from under the stairwell, then noticed Lez's stance and asked, "You plan on shooting him with your fingers?" "You know this dude?" Lez whispered to Cookie, changing her stance to a fighting stance.

Cookie nodded her head no.

"Is he the one that robbed you?" Lez asked.

"I'm not sure," Cookie started. "I told you I didn't get a look at him. He had on a mask and had a gun pointed in my face."

Lez watched the stranger reach in his pocket and pull out a phone, then spoke:

"You think you can steal my girl car, then bring it back like it's all good?"

Cookie noticed the phone he was holding was hers, so she asked, "How did you end up with my car?"

"And how did you know how to find my girl?" Lez interjected.

The stranger showed Cookie her phone, then tossed it to her.

"It's for you."

Cookie stared at her phone and noticed Ice's number pop up. She answered it slowly.

"How ya doing?" he began.

"I'm okay," she responded, not understanding how this guy and Ice link.

Ice informed her that he called her earlier, her line picked up, but she never acknowledged him. He told her he heard the whole situation as it was going down and that she did good by not doing nothing stupid and getting shot.

Cookie understood, but she didn't understand who this guy was and how he got her car back so fast.

Ice informed her that he has guys tailing her occasionally to ensure her safety and to protect his investment. He told her he received a call from Bobo, the guy standing before them, that she was being carjacked and that he gave the order to get her car back by any means necessary.

He ended with explaining to her how he was able to find where she was. Cookie smiled happily as Bobo pulled out her key fob and tossed it to her. *"My question to you is,"* Ice started as Cookie opened the car door and noticed her purse was in there, still intact, and more importantly, the bag of money was still there.

"How are you gonna handle this situation." "What you mean? I got my car back, and your money." She responded confused.

"Are you gonna let the guy get away that stole your car. What if next time, there is no one to get your belongings back."

Cookie pondered for a moment as Ice finished.

"Will you wait for the cops to figure it out."

She hadn't thought this through that far.

She wasn't prepared for this part of the game.

"How would you explain hundreds of thousands of dollars in the backseat of your car to the cops. Or better yet, what if you had cocaine in there. Will you admit that was your car and the contents within it?" "I guess I'ma put a word on the streets, and when I find him, I'ma handle it."

"I'ma do you one better. Put Bobo on the phone."

Cookie handed Bobo the phone, he nodded, handed Cookie back to the phone, then walked to her car, popped the trunk, then called her over to see what was inside.

In the trunk was the guy who stole her car. He was duct taped by the wrist and ankles, and he was brutally battered.

"So, what were you saying," Ice started. *"How was you gonna handle the guy who took your car when you see him?"*

The guy looked barely describable. Cookie almost felt sorry for him.

"It looks like you handled it already." She pleaded.

"Nah. That was just the warmup," Ice cut in.

"I need to know that if something like this or worse were to ever happen to my money or my product, You would be willing to ride or die. Ride or die, Cookie thought. She didn't feel she was willing to die for no drugs or money.

This was getting too out hand.

Lez on the other hand was excited to see the guy in that state. She was cursing and punching him, not caring of his condition.

"You want me to kill him?" Cookie asked.

Lez overheard that and jumped to it.

"KILL HIM! Hell yeah, I'll be right back!" she ran in the apt to retrieve a weapon.

"No!" Ice snapped. "I want YOU to want to kill him."

Cookie froze with Ice's response. She felt no harm was done. She wanted out, but she was already too far in.

"Would you have wanted him dead if he had gotten away?" Ice asked. Cookie had no answer. "Do you think this would have been a peaceful call if we talked and you tried to explain someone stole your car and a large amount of my money was taken too?"

Cookie still had no answer as Ice added, "Do you feel 'I'm sorry' would fix it? Or an 'I'll pay you back somehow' would resolve the problem?"

Cookie wanted to cry. She knew at that moment what her aunt was talking about. Ice was a man of business, nothing personal.

Lez came running back down the stairs carrying her trusted pink handgun. "Alright, I'm here!" she blurted, running to the trunk trying to get to the robber.

Bobo blocked her.

"She has to do it," Bobo cut in, turning toward Cookie.

He pulled out a large Dirty Harry–style gun that was almost as big as her. The shot would be very loud, bringing attention to the still-sleeping neighborhood.

She reached for Lez's trusted pink handgun. It was light and easy to handle. It was also the same gun she used to shoot the guy from Picketville.

She slowly raised the gun nervously.

The robber in the trunk's eyes slowly opened. He noticed Cookie holding the gun above him. He became quickly afraid, remembering her as the one whose car he had stolen not too long ago.

"Pop that clown!" Lez urged, noticing Cookie's hesitation.

"Give it to me, I'll do it," Lez pleaded, seeing the fear in the robber's eyes. "You ain't know who you were fucking with, huh nigga?"

Cookie stayed frozen; arm extended; gun cocked. But was unable to pull the trigger.

"He who hesitates, dies in battle," Ice preached through her earpiece. *"Kill or be killed."*

The more he talked, the angrier Cookie became. Ice didn't hear any gunshots, so he felt she was afraid, so he stated: *"This is a man's game. It's not for the faint of heart."*

Cookie started breathing heavy, trying to hype herself up. Catching eyes with the robber, she played back the event earlier. All she could see was him calling her out her name, forcing her out her vehicle, pointing his rifle in her face, keeping her purse, and driving off leaving her on the side of the road for dead.

She perked up, wiped a tear from the corner of her eye, then released six shots into his chest and face area.

Lez watched in proud amazement as Cookie let out a sigh of relief. This was her second body. She was starting to grow a stomach for this. Maybe she could handle this life after all.

Ice hung up with Cookie after he heard the gunshots and called Bobo. Bobo informed Cookie that Ice instructed him to take her car, dispose of the body, and return it later.

Cookie agreed, as her and Lez went back in the apt with a new outlook on life in the game. "Bitch, you ready now!" Lez stated proudly.

I am ready, Cookie thought, nodding in agreement.

She heard Lez in the background praising the way she handled the situation and how they are about to take over the streets. Cookie agreed.

Who the hell ever said this was a man's world? Cookie continued in thought. *The last time I remember, Beyoncé said, "Who run the world? and the answer was GIRLS.*

8

Ashes of the Crown

Detective Holzendorf received a call that he should report to the scene of a homicide. He informed them he worked with the drug unit, and homicide was not his department. The lead investigating officer told him this was something he needed to see, being that the victim was a C.I. he had working for him.

When he was told the address area, Det. Holzendorf hurried to the scene.

Police had the corner of Moncrief and Soutel blocked off with red tape. Flashing blue lights lit the skyline, helicopters hovered above in close proximity, the ambulance was on scene, but were too late.

A man lay dead on the ground in front of the Winn-Dixie parking lot as spectators looked from a distance. Several onlookers saw what happened, but at the same time, no one saw what happened as police asked around for any leads.

Det. Holzendorf got on the scene and noticed a body covered with a white sheet on the sidewalk. He didn't wait for the lead officer to escort him to the body; he went under the tape and walked over himself.

He placed on some latex gloves, took a deep breath, and pulled back the sheet. His worst thought was true. Josh, his snitch in the investigating murder of Rashod Williams, was dead from multiple gunshot wounds.

"MUTHA FUCK!" he snapped, shaking his head in disbelief.

"Hey, you!" an officer yelled from a distance. "Get away from there. Don't

71

contaminate my crime scene."

Det. Holzendorf stood up and turned toward the officer speaking. He immediately recognized Det. Holzendorf.

"Oh, it's you," the lead homicide detective, Rick Matthews, stated. "He was one of your guys, right?" he asked as Det. Holzendorf nodded."Have you gotten anybody to say anything?" Det. Holzendorf asked, looking around the crowd.

"You know how it is round these parts," Det. Rick started. "They see everything until the police ask have they seen anything."

"Or unless it happens to them," Holzendorf cut in.

"We do have one person who saw it all and wants to talk, but we got one problem."

"What's the problem?" Holzendorf asked.

"His momma won't let him talk."

"His momma!" Holzendorf snapped.

"How old is this guy?"

Det. Matthews scanned the area looking for this witness and his mother. He spotted him, called Det. Holzendorf over, then stated, "There he is right there!"

Det. Holzendorf watched this beautiful Black woman hover over this small kid, then Det. Matthews added, "And he's ten."

* * *

Cookie showed up to Club Heavy's carrying the duffel bag with the 20 kilos inside. Heavy personally met her outside and escorted her to his office.

Cookie handed Heavy the bag; he looked inside happily, then handed her the bag full of money.

"So, what you wanted to ask me?" he asked immediately as they sat down.

Cookie paused for a moment. She wondered if she would even get the truth from Heavy. After all, his real loyalty was to Tiger, not her.

"I found out some recent information that's bothering me, and I was hoping I could ask you a couple questions, so I'll know how to play it." "Oooookay,"

Heavy responded, confused.

"Was Lez pregnant with Tiger's babies?" Cookie asked, getting straight to the point.

"Whoa! Whoa! Whoa!" Heavy cut in, surprised. "Is who pregnant with what, now?"

Cookie sat up in the chair and repeated, "You heard the question. Was Lez ever pregnant with Tiger babies?"

"Lez ain't got no babies," Heavy chimed in. "Not that I know of."

He stared at Cookie's face and realized she believed this information she had, so he asked, "Where you get this information from?"

Cookie ignored his follow-up question and asked, "Was Tiger and Lez FUCKING?"

Heavy paused and thought for a moment. He realized dealing with women: when they ask certain questions, they already know the answer or majority of it; so he had to tread lightly before he incriminates himself or others. He decided to find out what she may already know first.

"Nah, man. Tiger my man. I woulda knew if some shit like that was going on," Heavy started. "Plus, Lez one of the homies. I don't even think she liked dudes like that."

"Nah, she definitely liked men," Cookie snapped back.

"Regardless of all that," Heavy cut back in, "my dawg was fucked up bout you."

"FUCKED UP BOUT ME!" Cookie yelled out. "I was locked up in jail for three and a half years and got not one letter from his ass."

Heavy sat and listened, watching Cookie become emotional as she continued.

"If anybody fucked up it was me," Cookie spoke, wiping a tear away.

"I fucked up for believing his bullshit all those years. I fucked up for taking the charge for him, thinking I'm doing a service for us. And lastly, I fucked up thinking I can come here and get the truth out of you."

Cookie stood up, about to leave, when Heavy stopped her.

"Come on, lil sis," Heavy started, walking around toward Cookie. "Alright, you want my truth? Here it is."

Heavy sat back on the edge of his desk as Cookie awaited his response.

"Do I feel Lez and Tiger got a lil too flirty at times? Yes. Do I feel they ever had sex? I can't confirm nor deny. Do I know anything about any baby or anybody being pregnant? Hell no."Cookie still had an angry look on her face as Heavy continued.

"But do I feel that Tiger loves you and only you with all his being?"

There was an awkward pause as Heavy stated, "I sure do."

Cookie sniffed and wiped her face again. Heavy walked over and hugged her while her mind was pondering all types of thoughts.

"I don't know where you got your information from, but they lying to you," Heavy added. Cookie knew the information was authentic; all this meeting did for her was confirm that Heavy didn't know about it.

Heavy again noticed Cookie wiping her face with her hand and directed her to his private bathroom. The door was hidden behind a fake bookshelf. It also doubled as a temporary hiding spot if being robbed or just not wanting to be bothered.

Cookie was in the bathroom, staring in the mirror at herself. Eyes red, snot leaking from her nose, and mascara running. She took a deep breath and mumbled, "Girl, get your shit together. You better than this."

She wiped her face and hands, smiled at her reflective image in the mirror, and was about to head back into the office with Heavy—until she heard a loud commotion. She assumed he was getting robbed with all the yelling and furniture crashing. She looked around the room to see if there was any way out from inside there. There wasn't any escape. She was a sitting duck. If they were to know about the hidden bathroom, she too might be dead.

Fifteen minutes had passed, the commotion had died down, and it seemed that whoever was outside was gone.

Cookie slowly cracked the door open to peek and see if the coast was clear. Before she could get a visual, the door flung open, and several men charged her with guns drawn. Her heart dropped; she felt death was inevitable.

"GET ON THE GROUND! GET ON THE GROUND!" she heard several of the guys command.

She obliged without hesitation. Body shaking, Cookie kept her eyes closed in fear she would be shot at any moment.

One of the gunmen stood her up and asked, "Who are you? And what are you doing here?"

Cookie opened her eyes and saw it was a room full of DEA agents. She noticed Heavy detained, standing by the door, another officer going through the duffel bag with the cocaine in it, while another was counting through the other bag with the money in it.

It was over for her and Heavy. This time for the long haul. She wanted to break down and cry, but at this point, what good would it do? She glanced over at Heavy, who looked defeated but held a straight face.

The officer asked again, "Who are you?"

Cookie had nothing.

Who would she tell them she was?

But before she could speak, Heavy chimed in, "She ain't nobody. She just some bitch I fuck with from time to time."

The officers glanced at Heavy, then back at Cookie, who had a scared look on her face. Her hands were raised in submission, and her head was facing downward, not wanting to directly stare at the men holding guns toward her.

"Is that true?" one of the officers asked.

Cookie quickly nodded. She would have confessed to being a prostitute if it would have gotten her out of that jam.

"Anyone else in there?" an officer asked as another officer walked over, inspecting the inside of the bathroom for any escape routes. "Take 'em downstairs."

The shit didn't work, Cookie thought.

Cookie watched as they placed Heavy in a blue UPS-style truck. They also had both of his security guards inside the truck also. She assumed they would place her inside a car by herself, being she was a female, but instead the officer asked how she got there. Cookie pointed at her car and was escorted to her vehicle by one of the officers.

"You need to find a better group of people to hang with," the lead DEA officer stated to Cookie as he opened her door for her to get in.

Cookie gave a fake nod and smile. She watched as the other officers placed the duffel bags with the money and drugs in them in the back of an unmarked Impala.

"What's ya name?" the agent asked, trying to flirt.

Cookie felt not flirting back would trigger the officer and he would find a reason to lock her up too. She put on her ghetto girl persona and responded, "KeKe."

"KeKe, huh?" the officer smiled.

Cookie nodded playfully. She was thinking of an active phone number she could give him because she knew he was about to ask for it. As she was anticipating being asked her number, the officer started chanting, "KeKe, do you love me; are you riding? Are you gonna be there beside me?"

Cookie's eyes widened. It took everything in her to keep from laughing. "You can't be serious!" she thought, watching the officer do the whole KeKe challenge"

This dude so green, she continued in thought.

"I gotta go," she spoke, cutting him off.

"Take down my number." She volunteered before she forgot the number she made up.

The officer placed her number in his phone, then asked, "Is the big guy your boyfriend or something?"

"Nah," Cookie quickly responded. "He just a dude I fux wit from time to time, ya know." Cookie tried to act as bubbleheaded as possible while talking to the officer. She really needed to sell the ghetto girl act.

"He gets my hair and my nails done, ya know what I'm saying."

"So he was your sponsor?" the officer asked, watching his guys wrap up the area, about to leave.

"So you THAT type chic?"

"What type of chic is THAT?" Cookie asked, trying not to get mad but stay in character.

"A prostitute!" Cookie blurted.

"Nah!" the officer quickly corrected. "You know, the type of girls that go after street guys with money. Then when he goes to jail, she on to the next one."

"That sounds exactly like a prostitute."

"Well, that's not what I meant," he ended nervously.

There was a brief awkward silence when Cookie cut in.

"Well, I gotta go, daddy. Hit me up later on."

The officer smiled and backed away as Cookie shut her door and drove off. She drove by the paddy wagon where the security and Heavy were still inside. Cookie caught eyes with Heavy as she passed. His head was down, and he looked as if it was all over for him.

She put her finger on her chin and pushed it upward, insinuating to him to keep his head up. The same sign he gave to her when she was in court. He nodded, lifted his head up, stuck his chest out, and Cookie drove away.

* * *

With Heavy being gone, Cookie was faced with a real dilemma. He moved over fifty percent of her product. Lez also moved over forty percent, and Cookie moved small amounts here and there to local small dealers.

The loss Cookie had at Heavy's club put a small dent in her finances. She not only lost the value of the 20 kilos, but she lost two hundred & twenty thousand dollars cash. That was part of her exit money for when she leaves the game. Now she has to make that up herself.

She hadn't planned on dealing with Lez until she got to the bottom of her and Tiger's story, but she had to play Lez like she felt Lez was playing her. It was a matter of hours, and the streets were in turmoil when they heard of Heavy's arrest.

Channel 9 News was on the scene not long after Cookie was let go. She made it home in time to see the traumatic ordeal being reported.

"I am Kimberly Longview reporting for Channel 9 News. As you can see behind me, a crowd of people was hoping to go inside this popular night spot, Club Heavy's. If you notice, JSO has the whole area taped off while DEA agents are inside."

"It was told to this reporter that the club owner, Heavy, whose real name is Mitchell Riles, was taken into custody for distribution of narcotics in a commercial dwelling. The DEA agents who made the arrest said that large amounts of cocaine and

large amounts of money were removed from the club and will be used as evidence. Apparently, Mr. Riles, or Heavy as the people know him, was using this known popular establishment as a front for an undercover drug ring.

"We interviewed a couple people to see how they feel about what's happening here tonight."

Cookie watched as it seemed the reporter hunted down the most incompetent people she could find to interview.

"Sir, what is your take on what transpired here tonight?"

She turned the camera to a guy who looked to have 32 gold teeth in his mouth, several obviously fake diamond chains, large unkept globs in his hair, oversized clothes, and some dirty knockoff Jordans.

"Well, ya know what I'm saying. I think it's fucked up. Oh—my bad, can I say fuck on TV?" "No, you can't," the reporter replied.

"Well, I think it's messed up how they did my dawg Heavy. He a good dude, ya know. I come to Club Heavy's all the time. After a long day of trapping, ya wanna come somewhere and chill, and Heavy's provide that."

"So, did you know Heavy personally?"

"Nah, not personally, ya know what I'm saying. But I seent him from time to time. He seemed skrate ta me. I just wish I woulda knew he was moving work like that. Shiiiiiid, I woulda asked him to put ya boy on."

"Okay." The reporter pulled the mic back to her when the interviewee asked to say one more thang.

She turned the mic back to him; he grabbed it with her and blurted, *"Holla at ya boi on Instagram at flipflop_trapguy. FREE MY NIGGA HEAVY!"*

He pushed the mic back to the reporter and walked off with his fist balled in the air chanting *"Free Heavy."*

"Did he say, flip flop underscore trap guy?" She tried to hold back a smirk as she continued.

"In other news, police have a break in the case in the murder of Joshua Williamson, whose body was found on the corner of Soutel and Moncrief. Sheila Kilpatrick has more. Sheila."

Cookie continued watching as the screen swapped from Club Heavy's to the Moncrief area.

"Thank you, Kimberly."
"I'm here on the corner of Moncrief and Soutel, where almost a week ago this was a crime scene."
"Murder victim Joshua Williamson was gunned down and pronounced dead here in this spot. Police didn't have any suspects until now."
"One brave person, who we are not at liberty to disclose, gave a vivid description of what he saw, and who he saw do it."
"Police had a sketch artist draw a picture of what the person said the suspect looks like."

Cookie watched the screen, and her eyes widened in awe as the sketch had an uncanny resemblance to Tiger.

"What the———." She paused as the reporter finished with:
"If anyone may know this person, or their whereabouts, we urge you to call Crime Stoppers. You can remain anonymous."

Cookie had seen enough. She turned the TV off and was about to take a shower. Before she got in, she heard her doorbell.
She froze for a moment.

What if it's the police, she thought. But she quickly debunked that thought because why would the police ring the doorbell?
The closer she got, she could see the silhouette of a short female. Ms. Baker.
"How ya doing, Ms. Baker?" Cookie asked, fatigued.
"I don't mean to disturb you this late, but I had to tell you— that man who came by before… he came by again."

Cookie stood there confused. Who was this guy that keeps popping up to her house? No one knew where she stayed. This was starting to get creepy.
"Thanks again, Ms. Baker," Cookie stated, about to shut her door.
"He gave me his card," Ms. Baker jumped in, stopping Cookie in mid stride.
Why didn't she start with that, old heffa, Cookie thought.
"He told me to give him a call when I see you come home."

Cookie grabbed the card as Ms. Baker added: "He was fine as hell. I may call him and tell him a prowler is in my house, and when he come inside, I'ma jump him. Put this tight ol' school nookie on him."

Cookie hadn't heard much of what Ms. Baker was saying. The name on the card had her spooked.

Detective MarkAnthony Holzendorf.

What did he want?

Why won't he leave her alone?

What had she done for him to hound her like this?

He was starting to become a thorn in her foot, and he had to be removed. But until then, she had bigger fish to fry.

How will she move all that work she had with Heavy being gone? How would she step to Lez about this Tiger situation? And lastly— but most importantly—Why did that sketch on TV look like Tiger?

9

Queen's Gambit

The streets were throwing a celebration of life party for Josh at Lonnie C. Miller Park. People from all sides of town came to the strip. Even the neighborhoods that were beefing with each other understood the laws of the streets. During funerals or family memorial services, there is a temporary truce. Too many innocent civilians.

This is usually the time where the big street kings come out to showcase their cars, jewelry, and status. Most of the family and close friends wear the T-shirt with the face of the deceased on the front. And no matter how evil the person was to the world, it's usually a caption in the background that reads Rest in Heaven with angel wings on their back.

Lez always warned Cookie that these are the type of events she should stay away from. The middle-class hustlers. These were the group of dealers that love to be seen flashing cash and driving loud, colorful cars with big rims.

Cookie had her own motive for showing up to the event. She knew she needed one or two more young, hungry hustlers she could sell these kilos to.

Parking her car and walking around, Cookie quickly saw what Lez was talking about. These guys were thirsty, trying to sleep with anything that moved. The girls that were there weren't leaving much to the imagination. They walked in packs like horny wolves in heat.

The guys that Cookie did stop to talk with only talked about their money, how they could take care of her, their cars, and how well they eat vagina.

"This was a waste of time," Cookie thought to herself. She was about to head back to her car and leave when she heard someone call her by name.

She looked around and noticed a guy who Tiger used to deal with.
"Heeeey. Umm. Umm—"
"Leon," the guy stated, seeing Cookie was struggling with his name.
"LEON!" she blurted with a smile. "How you been?"
"Same shit, different toilet," he started. "Who you out here with, 'cause this ain't your type of crowd."
"I know," she spoke, looking around at Sodom and Gomorrah.
"I didn't find what I was looking for, so I'm fenta go."
"How Tiger doing?" he began. "I been trying to reach him for the longest."
"So have we all," Cookie mumbled under her voice as Leon continued.
"Shit's ugly out here in these streets. Niggas selling trash dope right now. Nobody got that clean, clean."
"Really!" Cookie thought, trying to hold back her smile.

This is exactly what she been looking for. Young hungry hustler, not flashy, needing a supplier, and to add the icing to the cake: she knows him.

* * *

Detective Holzendorf was looking at the sketch of the guy who allegedly killed Joshua. He couldn't shake the fact that the image looked exactly like Tiger (Antonio McMillan).

He had yet to run across Tiger in years. He had seen Serena Loveless (Cookie) on many occasions and had heard her name in many conversations. He had also been to her house a couple times. He was sure Tiger purchased that house for her, being that she had not too long ago got out of jail. They were probably working together, he thought.

Cookie was wanted for questioning in the shooting murder of Tank (Rashod Williams), and Tiger was now wanted for questioning for the shooting murder of Josh, a close friend of Tank.

Detective Holzendorf decided to go talk to the witness who gave the sketch artist his description of the shooter. He wanted there to be no doubt that the

Tiger he has been after for years, and the man on the sketch, is indeed the shooter.

* * *

CLEVELAND ARMS APTS

Detective Holzendorf found the address to the witness who made the sketch and did an off-the-record visit.

"What are you doing at my house?" a lady blurted, answering through her broken screen door.

The detective could see a young kid on the couch playing on a tablet.

"Ima tell you like I told every other cop that came by here, I will not let my son testify, for no amount of money."

"Ms. Alexander, my name is Detective Mark Anthony Holzendorf."

"I don't give a shit what ya name is! The answer is no. No. NO! My son cannot testify."

"I'm not here to get ya son to testify or offer any money," the detective began, pulling pictures from his briefcase. "I just need your son to look at this picture and this sketch the officer drew and confirm that this is indeed the same person."

She looked at the pictures, then around at the crowd of people who were slowly crowding in the streets watching the interaction between her and Det. Holzendorf.

"Man. You can't be here, yo," she began. "These people round here don't take kindly to your kind. Then you gonna have them looking at me and my baby crazy. And if anybody coincidentally get busted for anything, they gonna think I snitched."

"Ma'am, please. A man was killed," the detective pleaded.

"And that's very unfortunate for him and his family," she added, not really caring at all, as she continued, "but the last thing I want is someone explaining to my family that me and my son was killed trying to help the police solve another murder."

"I understand your concern, ma'am, and all I need is for him to say this is the same guy he saw, and I will never bother you again."

The detective once again held up the pictures for the lady to see.

"I wish I could help you," she pleaded, slowly beginning to shut her door.

"That's Mr. Tony the Tiger."

"What was that?" Det. Holzendorf blurted, noticing her young son had come into the kitchen and saw him holding the pictures. "**TERRANCE, GO SIT YO ASS DOWN!**" his mom blurted, as the detective continued.

"Are you sure, young man?" Holzendorf asked with a smile.

The young man nodded, and the detective quickly placed his pictures back in his briefcase. "Here, this is my card." He reached out his card, but she was reluctant to take it—until she realized she may need it being her son made a statement.

"I swear on my life, if someone as much as knock on your door hard, you give me a call."

The mom shut the door without giving the detective any response. When the detective got back to his car, a few of the neighborhood bad boys shouted, "You in the wrong area, Officer, this 50-20. Cops ain't allowed in here unless we call you to come pick up the body."

"Is that right?" the detective asked, turning to face the young crowd.

"First off, it's Detective, jit. And I grew up in Brentwood and the Blodgett Homes. So what you saying don't impress me. This era here is sweet compared to the era I grew up in," the detective commented with a smirk on his face. "So you may wanna walk off, while you still have the ability to walk." There was dead silence as the detective got in his car and drove off.

* * *

Lez had been trying to reach Cookie but to no avail. She had no clue that Cookie was in attack mode and was dodging Lez for her best interest.

Lez remembered Cookie renting her own little stash spot in Sherwood. It was supposed to be where she kept her product and cash so she wouldn't have to drag drugs and money back and forth from her actual residence.

Lez pulled up to the house and noticed Cookie's Audi R8 and the new Cadillac CT5 outside as well. At first glance, Lez thought that Cookie was being robbed—or worse, dead.

But seeing the style of vehicles out front, she thought only one thing: Tiger finally showed up, and Cookie was inside getting her hips dislocated and her back blown out.

"That's why she didn't answer the phone," Lez mumbled with a smile.

Lez felt a **tad bit jealous**, reminiscing on the days Tiger would blow her back out. But Cookie was her girl now, so she could no longer envision Tiger in that way.

Lez sat in her car playing on her phone, giving the love birds some time to reconnect.

A few minutes passed, and Lez noticed Cookie's front door open. Cookie and a young guy came out smiling and joking.

"Oookaaay!" Lez said jokingly.

"I see ya, Stella. Gone get ya groove back, girl."

She watched as Cookie happily waved while the young guy drove off. Lez got out of the car as she and Cookie caught eyes.

"I guess I need to get me a YN too, huh?" Lez joked. "I wanna smile like he had you smiling."

Cookie's smile turned to a frown quickly as Lez approached the porch. Cookie turned to walk back inside the house, and Lez was close behind her.

"Girl, I been calling you for the past few days," Lez started. Cookie gave no response.

"Who was that sexy young thang that just left outta here?" Lez continued, but Cookie still gave no response.

"What's up with you? You alright?"

"What you want, Lez?" Cookie shot back with an attitude.

"Uh uhm, Bitch!" Lez snapped. "What's wrong with you?"

Cookie stared at Lez, eyes blazing.

Cookie wanted to scream out, "**YOU WHAT'S WRONG WITH ME, HOE! You been fucking my man and was pregnant by him!**"

But instead, she stated, "Been a long day."

"I know what you mean, girl," Lez said, walking toward the kitchen to get herself a drink.

"The streets getting crazy now that Heavy gone."

Cookie watched as Lez walked around her place like it was her own. She wanted to release the fire burning inside her as Lez continued."And my friend Josh, whose house I took you to when you got out," Lez explained, "I found out he dead. They had a memorial for him and everything."

This wasn't new information to Cookie. She just wanted Lez to get to the point and leave before they ended up having a memorial for her as well.

"I'm bout done with the game; the streets don't respect the code anymore. These dudes rather go to war than get money. They rather buy a gun and rob you than buy an ounce of coke and hustle."

Although Cookie wasn't interested, she had to admit Lez made sense. What was she doing it for? When would it end?

She had already been robbed and could've been killed over a car. They would definitely kill her over drugs and money. She made a vow to herself that after this load Ice gave her, she was done.

She had come to the realization that Tiger was gone for good. He wasn't dead as she thought, because that sketch was definitely him. She had to move on and be okay with that.

After a few more minutes of Lez venting about the change in the game, she finally told Cookie she needed 20 kilos.

During the exchange, there was a knock at the door. Lez went to answer it.

"Daaaaamn, Chica," Lez said, noticing the guy at the door. "You know a lot of fine YN's."

Cookie looked out and saw it was Leon, the young man she met at Lonnie C. Miller Park.

"Let him in," Cookie said calmly, sorting out the five kilos Leon requested.

"Heeeeey," Lez flirted as Leon brushed past her."How you doing?" she continued.

"I'm fine."

"Yes, you are," Lez added, staring at Leon's backside.

"Don't you have somewhere to be?" Cookie asked, noticing Lez acting out of character.

"I'm right where I need to be."

"Bye, Lez!" Cookie snapped with a straight face.

Lez closed the door as Cookie addressed Leon with a smile.

"You gotta excuse her," Cookie commented. "But she hasn't had any in a while."

"Oh, is that right," Leon cut in, looking back at the door. "Well, she can definitely get it."

Cookie and Leon walked toward the kitchen where Cookie had the five kilos placed on the table.

* * *

Lez was almost a mile down the road when she realized she left her phone in Cookie's spot. She made a U-turn and headed back.

When she got back to Cookie's spot, she could hear commotion on the inside. She didn't have her gun on her, but she did have her stun gun. She crept onto the porch and could hear Cookie being tossed around.

Lez panicked. If she ran in without a plan, they both would be in trouble, especially if he had a gun. Her phone was inside, so she couldn't call for help. By the time she ran down the block to the neighbor, Cookie may be dead.

She decided to charge in. Whatever happens, happens. She flung the door open and burst in like a bull in a China shop. She saw Cookie sprawled on the floor, face bruised and bloody. Leon was bagging the kilos that were on the table.

"YOU SON OF A BITCH!" Lez yelled, attacking Leon with her Taser.

Leon looked up, dropped the bag, and when Lez got close enough, he swung and knocked her unconscious.

An hour had passed when Lez finally became conscious. She noticed she was still in Cookie's spot. Her head was throbbing, and the house was quiet and empty. She looked in every room, hoping to find Cookie. The house was a mess, and the bags with the dope and money in it were gone.

The bright side of the whole ordeal was, Lez saw her phone on the counter by the refrigerator. She didn't know who to call. If she called the police, they would come, look for clues, ask all type of questions, search, and may or may not find drug paraphernalia.

She ran outside to see if her car was still there. It was. The keys were still in the ignition, and the car was still running.

Cookie's car was gone; and so was Leon's.

He had to have an accomplice, she thought.

Who was he? Where did they go? And why did he take Cookie?

Lez's mind was going a mile a minute. She didn't know what to do at this point. This was bad. It dawned on Lez she had one person she could call. He told her only in case of an emergency to give him a call.

This was definitely an emergency.

She went to her contacts and chose the name titled "Emergency Only."

The phone rang several times, then someone picked up. There was no voice on the other end, just some light breathing. Lez knew the person on the other end was listening, so she took a deep breath and stated, "It's me, Tiger. I got some bad news."

10

The Resurrection

Heavy was being held in the Pre-Trial Detention Facility in Downtown Jacksonville. The DEA was looking to build a solid case on Heavy, and they felt they had enough to do so, but they wanted more arrests.

Over the years that they had been watching Heavy's activities, they were able to make several smaller arrests; but nothing to get them the big score. His accounts and tax records were lined up to show that his income was coming from Club Heavy's.

They needed to show video surveillance and gather witnesses to take him down, and prove his club was a front for laundering his drug money. When Heavy's close friend PieYay died, it almost gave Heavy an escape route.

PieYay was a lot flashier, and the DEA knew he was a street runner, so they started investigating Heavy's documents to see if he was laundering large amounts of drug money thru his club for he and PieYay. The DEA was planning on crashing down on PieYay before his death and bringing an indictment against Heavy.

The case was weak at the time, so they needed more. The DEA finally got access to a pair of inside eyes. Steve from Heavy's security detail was stopped for a DUI. This would be on record as his third DUI. He was a two-time convicted felon, and a gun was found under the passenger seat of the car he was driving. To make matters worse, his license was suspended for tickets and failure to appear.

He agreed to cooperate in exchange for no jail time. He helped build years of valuable evidence to show Heavy was indeed moving large amounts of cocaine out of his club. Unfortunately, they were never able to determine who was his connect.

Heavy was brought from his unit down to the Police Memorial Building for questions by the DEA.

"Being that you gonna be here for a while, we hope that you are finding your accommodations here at the Jacksonville Detention Hotel fit to your liking," one of the officers asked sarcastically as Heavy entered the room.

"The eggs were a lil lumpy this morning," Heavy snapped back, sitting at the table.

"I'll alert the cook. I'm sure he'll put extra piss in it for you next time; to take the lumps out."

Heavy didn't bother to respond to the comment. He sat quietly for a few seconds, waiting for someone to speak.

"Man, what am I down here for?" Heavy asked, breaking the silence.

"You got somewhere to be? You plan on opening ya club tonight?" the officer joked.

"I was expecting a conjugal visit from ya wife. Didn't wanna miss that."

The officer tried to charge at Heavy but was held back by another officer.

"You got plenty of time for that," the officers confirmed to each other.

As Heavy was feeling this meeting was getting uncomfortable, two DEA agents walked inside.

"We got it from here, gentlemen," they started with the officers, holding the door open for them. "We'll call you if we need you."

Heavy held the middle finger up to the cops as they left the room.

"You may wanna build an ally with the cops, being you gonna be here for a long while," the agent started.

"Ya think so, huh?" Heavy spoke calmly.

"Abso-fucking-lutely!" the agent confirmed, placing his folder on the desk.

"You fucked, big man."

"With a really big dick," the second agent added. "What yall want, man? I gotta get back to my dorm," Heavy spoke with an attitude.

"We thought ya may wanna help yaself," the first agent spoke.

"Shit don't look good for ya, buddy. Help us, help you."

"Help yall help me, huh?" Heavy spoke sarcastically, glancing at both agents with an evil grin.

"What if I say kiss my entire ass."

"If you ever wanna see the light of day again, I wouldn't suggest u say that," agent one stated. "We trying to give your ass a lifeline. You need to take it. 'Cause if you don't, we going for the max," agent two added.

Heavy gave a slight pause then stated, "I'll pass." He stood up, insinuating he was done talking. The agents called for the JSO officers to come and get Heavy to escort him back to lock up.

As he was walking out, agent one stated, "You know you making a big mistake, right."

Heavy looked at the JSO officers escorting him, then back at the DEA agents, then blurted,

"Kiss. My. En-Tire-Ass."

* * *

"Wake up Princess." Leon stated lightly slapping Cookie in the face.

Cookie slowly opened her eyes. Face sore, and body weak from being beaten on, and lack of food.

"You don't look so hot, queen pin," Leon mocked, staring at Cookie's bruised eye. "If you leave here alive, you may wanna get that looked at."

Cookie didn't respond, she was trying to get comfortable. She had been tied to a chair for hours, and her body was numb.

"I have to pee," Cookie pleaded.

"I don't give a fuck if you gotta deliver a baby. Ya ass ain't moving til I get what I want!"

"What do you want?" Cookie asked, trying to endure through the pain. "I'm

sure you took the dope I had for you. And if you want money, I got money."
"You think this is what this is about?" Leon snapped. "FUCKING MONEY!"

He walked over to Cookie and clasped her chin in his hand, forcing her to look at him. "FUCK YOUR MONEY! This is about family.""What family? What are you talking about?" Cookie whined.

"My cousin, Josh."

"Josh!" Cookie cut in. "I don't know any Josh. And what does he have to do with me? What did I do to him?"

"Oh, not you, Princess."

Leon walked away and grabbed a bottled water from the counter and walked back toward Cookie.

"You look parched."

He opened the water and squeezed it into her face. He laughed as she coughed and gagged, then he poured the remainder on top of her head.

"It's your boyfriend I'm after."

"Who? Tiger?" Cookie got out between coughs. "Yeeeeah. Tiger!" Leon said with a devilish look. "I'll exchange your life for his."

"I haven't talked to Tiger in years, I swear," Cookie pleaded in tears.

"THAT'S BULLSHIT! I asked you at the park how was he, and you said he was fine. So, you better call him and get him here, or it's a wrap for you."

"PLEASE! I SWEAR ON MY LIFE, I HAVEN'T SPOKEN TO TIGER IN ALMOST FOUR YEARS." "Well, that's unfortunate for you."

Leon grabbed his gun, walked over to Cookie, and pointed his gun to her head.

"Can I at least know what he did to make you wanna kill me?" Cookie begged, eyes squinting, bracing for the gunshot.

Leon hesitated, ready to pull the trigger. He decided he would give her this last request.

"He killed my cousin Josh."

Cookie began to breathe heavy, thinking this was all he would tell her.

"Left him lying dead in the middle of the street like some dog."

Leon grabbed Cookie by the throat and began to squeeze.

"Apparently, he calls himself tying up loose ends. It was said that my cousin was supposed to testify against you and some bitch for killing his homeboy at his house."

Leon released her throat when he noticed she began to blackout.

"Witnesses say a blue SUV turned the corner where my cousin was standing and opened fire. No words, no confrontation, no fight, just fye fye fye."

"How do you know it was Tiger?" Cookie mumbled.

"Bitch, I ain't stupid. Everybody knows his truck. Plus, people saw him and gave a sketch of the nigga to the news."

Cookie remembered that night. She didn't believe that was Tiger, nor understood why he would kill someone in public if he was trying to stay low key.

"This don't have anything to do with me," Cookie pleaded. "This between you and Tiger." "Nah, Princess. That nigga killed my cousin for you. So, Ima kill you for my cousin."

He raised his gun up toward Cookie's head. Her eyes closed, and tears flowed rapidly down her face.

"Even swap, no swindle," he added as he was about to pull the trigger.

BOOM!

The front door of Leon's house was kicked in. Two masked intruders entered with guns drawn. Leon stepped back and turned his gun toward the invaders. Alas, he wasn't fast enough; they had the drop on him.

Both gunmen opened fire, releasing countless projectiles from the AR-15 and 9mm they were holding. Cookie was so in shock, her heart couldn't take the activity, that she passed out. When she woke up, she was face to face with Tiger. He was holding her head up, smiling. The light behind his head gave off the silhouette of a halo and an angelic light.

"Am I dead?" Cookie wondered, feeling this was judgement and she was at the pearly gates.

"No. You're not dead," Tiger responded, showing off his pearly whites.

"So, this is real? And you're really here?"

"Yes, I'm here. I'm really here."

Tiger was excited. Cookie was in shock, especially to be alive.

"Wow!" she mumbled.

She took a deep breath, closed her eyes, opened them slowly, looked up at Tiger once again, then slapped him with all her might.

"You've been alive and around this whole time and you pick this moment to pop the hell up."

Tiger sat Cookie up. He was in awe that she slapped him, but he understood. He began to try to explain his whole hiding ordeal. She was mad; one could say, even pissed. But she was happy at the same token. This would take two lifetimes for him to make up.

He helped her to her feet, and as she was about to embrace him, the second gunman came from out the back.

"The rest of the house is clear. No one else is in here."

"LEZ!" Cookie blurted out.

"What's up, baby girl? You okay?"

Cookie stood stunned. What the hell was going on? Maybe she was dead for real but went to Hell instead.

"How did y'all find me? And more importantly, how are y'all two together?"

"Your car GPS," Lez cut in.

"And Lez called me and said she think you were kidnapped," Tiger added.

"LEZ CALLED YOU!" Cookie snapped. "YOU KNEW HOW TO REACH HIM THIS WHOLE TIME?"

Lez had nothing to say. She glanced at Tiger, then back at Cookie. She wanted to escape the situation. In her mind, she was only doing what she was asked.

Tiger tried to hug Cookie to calm her down, but she was not in the state of mind to accept affection. She wanted blood.

"DON'T FUCKING TOUCH ME!" she yelled, pushing away.

"You two been playing in my face like I'm some handicapped blind bitch!"

"What are you talking about?" Tiger asked, then continued. "YES, I had to stay far away from you in fear the Feds were still watching. And YES, Lez had my contact number but was only told to call in a dying emergency while shit dies down. And YES, I couldn't visit or write you in jail 'cause they read those letters. And YES, I am sorry for everything you been going thru. But I have been watching and protecting you from a distance."

Cookie stared at Tiger with an evil eye. She felt her face, then looked around at her surroundings.

"Is this what you call protecting me?" she huffed angrily. "I've been robbed, fondled, beat on, and kidnapped, and you call this protecting me!"

Tiger had no response. Cookie had made a valid point. The situation was not how Tiger hoped it would play out. He never anticipated this life for he nor Cookie.

Lez continued to stay silent. She knew she didn't have a dog in this fight.

"And answer me this," Cookie started, staring at Tiger then at Lez. "Since you admitted that yes, you did this, and yes, you did that…"

Tiger stood at attention as Cookie asked, "Are you two fucking?"

Lez's mouth dropped to the floor; Tiger's eyes widened, wondering where Cookie would get such a question from.

"And before y'all decide to lie, just know—" she glanced over at Lez and added, "I read your letter. You know, the one you had encased in the glass."

Lez stood froze. She couldn't do or say anything to clear this one up.

"Yeah." Cookie nodded, watching their reactions. "The letter to your unborn babies. The one that you signed at the end: 'Love Mommy and Daddy, Leslie Hill and Antonio McMillan.

There was dead silence. A tear dropped from Cookie's eyes. She felt used, she felt broken, but mostly she felt stupid.

"I knew in the back of my mind you were fucking some bitch," Cookie snapped at Tiger, who was standing there looking dumbfounded. "But you…" She turned her attention toward Lez. "You came off as my friend, fed me all that bullshit about loyalty and friendship, and the whole time you were fucking my piece of shit man."

"I can explain," Lez mumbled sadly.

"BITCH, DO IT LOOK LIKE I WANNA HEAR WHAT YOU GOTTA SAY?"

She tried to attack Lez, but Tiger intervened. She was kicking and clawing, trying to break free.

"LET ME GO!" Cookie yelled, shaking free from Tiger's grip.

Lez was feeling so embarrassed and ashamed that she turned and rushed out.

Cookie began to cry more hysterically. Tiger once again tried to console her.

"DON'T FUCKING TOUCH ME! I HATE YOU." "You don't mean that," Tiger responded, feeling destroyed.

"Oh, I absolutely do." Cookie spoke, placing her palm on Tiger's face and mushing him. "You are a heartless, careless, selfish, deadbeat ass nigga. And I don't wanna see you ever again."

Cookie stared at Tiger for a brief moment. He said nothing. This was not how she envisioned their meeting, but it was things that had to be said. She was a new woman, a stronger woman, an independent woman.

Cookie walked past Tiger feeling like the Queen of England. She noticed the bag Leon stole with the kilos in it, and the bag with her money inside also. She had a decision to make. Was that worth the turmoil her life had been going thru? Lez told her people don't respect the rules of the game anymore.

She took a deep breath, rolled her eyes, walked toward the door and mumbled, "I'm done with this shit. They can have it."

"Come here!" Tiger commanded, watching Cookie standing by the door. She was angry, bruised up, and ready to go.

"I don't got time to play with you," she snapped with her arms crossed.

"I said come here." He walked up behind her.

She breathed heavy, feeling Tiger rub up close against her.

"I hate you," she repeated. But this time he could tell there was hurt and hope in her voice.

"I know." He eased down and kissed her on the back of her neck. "I'm sorry."

She wasn't letting him off this easy, but her body longed for him. Her anger intensified her lust for him. He pushed her up against the wall, removed her bottoms, and made love to her standing.

After they were done, no words were exchanged. Cookie pulled up her clothes and brushed herself off.

"Don't think this changes anything," Cookie demanded. "Consider that as a reminder of what you'll never be getting again."

She walked toward the door and stated, "I meant what I said. I'm done with you."

11

Til Death Do Us Part

Detective Holzendorf had been driving throughout different neighborhoods looking for Tiger. He was determined to not let Josh's murder become a cold case. Tiger was gonna answer for the laws he'd been breaking.

Det. Holzendorf was getting tired and figured he'd call it a night. He decided he had a taste for fried shrimp and oysters from Tunis. As he was driving, he noticed a couple having an aggressive dispute.

He continued past, not wanting to deal with any paperwork if it ended up being more than it seemed. He couldn't help but glance over at the couple, being that the woman was the aggressor, and the guy didn't seem to be a threat.

Det. Holzendorf had to do a double take when he got a good look at who the two people were. "What the hell!" he yelled, spinning his head back quickly and losing control of the wheel. He swerved into oncoming traffic, then hard back into the proper lane. He turned the steering wheel too far, the car jumped the curb and ran headfirst into a tree.

He took a few seconds to gather his emotions, then moved his body slowly to assure he didn't have any broken bones or soreness. He glanced back and saw who looked to be Tiger and Cookie.

He opened his door quickly and tried to get out swiftly, forgetting to unfasten his seat belt. Although Tiger and Cookie had an angry quickie inside Leon's house, he was still trying everything to get Cookie to understand his side of the story.

All she mentioned was how she felt that he and Lez set her up to go to prison so they could continue sleeping together. As they were arguing, they witnessed a car lose control and run into a tree.

"Oh my God," Cookie spoke, concerned.

Tiger watched momentarily. He was about to go help until he saw the driver's door fling open.

"He alright," he spoke calmly.

"You sure? Go see?" Cookie added.

Tiger was considering going over until he noticed the driver.

"Is that—"

"TIGER!" Det. Holzendorf screamed from down the road.

"That is that son of a bitch," Holzendorf mumbled to himself.

He attempted to charge across the street to make those arrests. Several cars kept stopping and blocking his crossing to see if he was okay.

"MOVE YOUR VEHICLES, DAMNIT!" he yelled.

Tiger watched as Holzendorf pulled out his gun and started across the street.

"That's Detective Holzendorf!" Tiger blurted out loud. "RUUUUUN!" he yelled, then turned back toward Cookie, who had already noticed the Detective and was already running.

She was so startled that it didn't dawn on her she was running the opposite direction of where her car was parked.

"Where are you going?" Tiger screamed, chasing behind her. "Your car is the other way!"

Cookie stopped and looked around, giving Tiger time to catch up to her.

"Your car. Is in. The other. Direction," Tiger spat out, trying to catch his breath. Cookie looked down one street then the other. She couldn't tell one block from the other. This wasn't her side of town; all the new constructed houses looked the same to her.

"Which way do we go?" she spoke in a panic.

"Back that way." Tiger pointed in the opposite direction, toward the same direction Holzendorf was coming.

They got off the main road and hid behind an abandoned-looking house. The dogs barking in the yard a few houses down were clearly gonna give up their position. They were sure an abandoned-looking house would be the first place Holzendorf would look.

There was yet to be any sign of Holzendorf in the area. They both listened to hear if any police sirens or helicopters were in the distance. Everything seemed clear.

Maybe he decided not to chase them and went back to his car for help, Tiger thought.

"We need to go three blocks over, in that direction." He once again pointed in the area where the Detective was seen.

"You ready?" Tiger asked, about to run out.

"Hold up." Cookie stopped him, seeming nervous.

She paused, staring at Tiger for a brief moment.

"What is it?" he blurted, anxious, looking out in the clear area.

"Do you love her?" Cookie asked with a sad face.

"WHAT! WHO?"

"Lez," Cookie cut in quickly. "Do you love her?"

Cookie feared Tiger's answer. Lez was beautiful, independent, street smart, and Cookie knew she loved Tiger.

"We can't talk about this later? We got some shit going on right now."

"It's a yes or no answer," Cookie chimed in quickly.

After a brief pause, Tiger touched her face and stated, "Babe, I love you. Now come on, we gotta go."

Cookie watched as Tiger surveyed the area to make sure it was clear. She also noticed he never confirmed nor denied loving Lez.

But he was right, they had to go.

The area was too quiet. It was as if no one was home at none of their houses. The dogs that were barking earlier had even stopped.

"Let's go," Tiger spoke, guiding Cookie from behind the abandoned house and through a small path heading to the next block. That street was also clear. They made a run for it again.

They were one block away. Tiger could see the house where Cookie's car was. When they got near, Tiger could see a couple of police cruisers. The officers were talking to the neighbor across the street from the house where Cookie was being held captive.

He noticed the neighbor occasionally pointing at the house where Cookie's car was parked. Tiger could only assume the neighbor was telling the cops about the activity that happened earlier.

That thought was confirmed when one of the officers walked over, walked around Cookie's car, then onto the porch.

"FUCK!" Tiger huffed softly.

"What? What's going on? What's the hold up?" Cookie asked nervously.

Tiger pulled her next to him and pointed through the bushes at the scene he saw. "No, no, noooo!" Cookie responded, repeating This is bad over and over again."Let me think," Tiger blurted after Cookie kept asking, What are we gonna do?

It was too late to try to figure out how to get her car. Eventually, after the cops found Leon's body in the house, the area would be really swarmed with cops.

They had to leave, and fast.

"We not that far from Lonni C. Miller," Tiger stated, convinced. "If we can get there, we can slip thru the back way and be in Ken Knight within minutes."

Cookie had no idea of the area Tiger was talking about. This was his domain, so she had no choice but to trust him.

They began walking down the street, trying to blend in as a regular couple out for a stroll.

The plan was seeming to work. They could see Lonni C. Miller off in the distance. Tiger began to pick up the pace as Cookie followed.

"Oh my God, we're almost there," Cookie stated with a smile.

"Try to keep up," Tiger blurted, crossing the street.

They could vaguely hear someone calling their name from a distance. They looked around to see if it was someone they knew; hopefully they could get a ride.

Looking harder, Tiger noticed it was Det. Holzendorf chasing after them on foot pursuit.

"This nigga will not give up!" Tiger said, agitated.

He started to run as Cookie stayed close behind.

POW! POW!

Tiger ducked and dodged, hearing gunshots close by.

"Babe! HE SHOOTING AT US!" Cookie stated in a panic.

"FREEEEEZE!" Det. Holzendorf screamed, running down the street pointing his gun.

"Fuck this," Tiger snapped, pulling out his gun he was carrying. "I'm done fucking with this nigga."

"What are you fenta do?" Cookie asked, concerned, seeing Tiger turning back about to walk toward Holzendorf's direction.

"You keep heading toward the park," Tiger stated, pushing Cookie away. "I got this." POW! POW! POW!

Tiger returned fire toward Holzendorf.

Holzendorf dove to the ground, aimed at Tiger, and released two more shots in their direction. Tiger screamed out and dropped to one knee. He had been hit in the left shoulder by one of Holzendorf's bullets. "Tiger, come on!" Cookie pleaded, seeing he dropped to his knees.

"I SAID LEEEEEAVE!"

Cookie backed away slowly, watching Tiger stand back on his feet.

POW! POW!

Tiger returned fire at Holzendorf.

Cookie watched as the Detective and Tiger exchanged gunfire for what seemed like forever.

Onlookers watched as Tiger dropped once again. One of Holzendorf's bullets hit Tiger in the abdomen.

"NOOOOOO!" Cookie screamed as tears dropped from her face.

She watched Holzendorf get closer to Tiger with his gun still drawn.

"Drop your weapon," Holzendorf demanded, seeing Tiger lying on the ground, but his gun was clenched in his hand.

Tiger glanced up at Holzendorf. This was the closest they'd been to each other in over four years.

"I finally got your ass," Holzendorf stated with a grin. "Now, I said drop your weapon."

Tiger watched as Holzendorf held a tight grip on his weapon, still pointing at him. Tiger's breathing became harder and more faint with each inhale.

Holzendorf noticed Tiger slowly fidgeting with his weapon.

"Don't you do it," the Detective warned, anticipating Tiger's thoughts. "It's over. Drop your weapon!"

Tiger's eyes veered over to Lonni C. Park. He couldn't see Cookie, so he assumed she had got away.

He didn't know Cookie was hiding behind a bush, witnessing the whole ordeal. He smiled in the area Cookie was in. She felt he could see her, or sense she was watching.

"I love u," he lip-synced.

"I love u more, baby," Cookie mumbled back, face full of tears.

"I'm not going to jail," Tiger mumbled to Det. Holzendorf.

"Don't do it, man. It ain't—"

Before the Detective could finish his statement, Tiger clasped his gun then tried to turn it onto Holzendorf.

"STOOOOOP!" Holzendorf yelled before discharging three shots into Tiger's chest.

Holzendorf watched as Tiger's gun dropped from his hand. He eased in closer and kicked his gun away from him. Holzendorf stared down at Tiger's body.

He was dead.

Cookie watched in horror as Holzendorf ended Tiger's life before her eyes. Her heart crumbled, remembering less than an hour ago she was telling Tiger she hated him and wanted him out of her life forever.

There was nothing she could do at this point. If she ran out to be with Tiger, she would surely be arrested, and Tiger's death would have been in vain. She looked behind her in the park. She had no real idea where she was, but she remembered what Tiger told her.

She followed the trail in the park. It led her to the front entrance, which was less than a five-minute walk to Ken Knight, where she knew people who would help.

Holzendorf made the 911 call from his cellphone. He informed them of who he was, and they dispatched his information through. He stated shots were fired, a man was down, and they needed an emergency EMT unit. It wasn't long before the area was swarmed with cops and an ambulance.

Holzendorf explained his version of the situation. He informed the lead officers of who Tiger was, the shots each of them fired, and the fact there was still a suspect at large. A woman.

He wasn't giving too much information because this was his case after all. The evidence officers were placing tag numbers next to every shell they found.

Holzendorf walked over to the gun Tiger used. He was curious about something Tiger said.

"I'm not going to jail."

Why would he say that when he was clearly outgunned? Holzendorf thought. Unless... Holzendorf knelt down, picked up Tiger's gun, and dislodged the clip. Empty. Holzendorf shook his head. His thought was true.

Tiger forced Holzendorf to shoot him by going for his gun. He knew he didn't have any more bullets. But he chose death over life in jail.

Cookie had one of the neighborhood residents drive her by the area where everything had just transpired.

Soutel was blocked with police cars and red tape, indicating someone was dead. Cookie could see from a distance Tiger's body lying on the ground. She could also see Holzendorf laughing and joking with an officer like all was golden.

Vengeance was in her eyes. She waited over four years to reunite with Tiger, and with a twisted turn of fate, she met him and lost him all in the same day.

Cookie had the driver take her across town to her house. She had to get some affairs in order. She couldn't leave the game at this point if she wanted to.

Too much had happened, and too many people had died. Her name and involvement in certain cases guaranteed there would be many restless nights.

Cookie called Ice and told him of her dilemma. He gave her the number to a monster lawyer who won many high-profile cases. She also told him of the major losses she'd taken in a matter of weeks. She informed him of Heavy's arrest, Lez and her falling out, and Tiger's death.

"This a grown man's game," Ice informed her. "Losses are inevitable."

She told Ice she was bowing out before her number was called.

They set up a meeting so she could pay Ice what she owed him for the losses. That would leave her with enough to pay the large amount the lawyer would want for retainer, enough to relocate to a smaller place, and maybe a few dollars for a Whopper combo with cheese.

Standing in the shower letting the water trail down her back, Cookie reminisced about her time with Tiger, past and present. She smiled and cried at the same time. She felt if they'd left earlier, he'd still be alive. If they weren't arguing outside, he'd still be alive. If they waited to have sex, he'd still be alive.

Regardless of what transpired today, Tiger was the love of her life.

She would never see him again. She would always envision the last time they were intimate was when they had angry sex.

Channel 9 News was reporting on the death of Tiger, according to Det. Holzendorf's interpretation of how the event went down.

Kimberly Longview interviewed him and some of the bystanders of the event earlier today. Everyone made Tiger out to be some kind of vigilante trying to kill law enforcement. Cookie watched as the cops painted Tiger as a rabid dog that had to be put down. The community that he took care of made it seem as if the neighborhood would now be better off.

Cookie shook her head, then turned the TV to her favorite show, The Big Bang Theory. She cried herself to sleep, knowing she'd have to plan the memorial service of the man she vowed to always love.

One thing she could say about their crazy situation was: it truly was 'Til Death Do Us Part.

12

The Weight of the Crown

A week had passed, and Cookie alerted the immediate family of Tiger's death. The streets knew the same night, and the race for who would be the next Kingpin had started. The streets were dry since Heavy was gone, Lez stopped coming in the hood much, and Cookie didn't wanna be in the game any longer.

Tiger's funeral was this coming Saturday, and she had to get a big enough venue to fit all the people she knew would come—not just to pay their respects; most were there to be nosey and have something to gossip about.

It seemed the whole world was wearing different shirts with Rest in Heaven images of Tiger on the front. Some of the same people who were in front of the camera saying the world may be better now were in Facebook and Instagram chats saying how much they would miss him.

Cookie hadn't talked to Lez, and for good reason. She couldn't guarantee she could hold her tongue. But it was a little disappointing to her that Lez hadn't reached out to say anything about Tiger's death—being they both saw him on his last day alive.

At the same time the world was mourning Tiger's death, the story of Leon's death was being televised also. The news was outside his house showing the surrounding area. Cookie noticed her car was still parked in the same spot. No one had yet to reach out about who the owner was, why it was there, or its involvement.

Although Cookie loved that car and wanted it back, it brought her too much grief. Getting it back and selling it crossed her mind, but she didn't want any parts of it, period.

The body viewing was a success. People came through in large groups. As was expected, people were overdramatic when seeing Tiger in the casket. Tiger had all his arrangements taken care of when he was alive.

His casket was white pearl with gold handles and gold trimming around the bedding. A life-sized picture of himself, taken at Club Heavy, was displayed on a large mantle. His suit was white also; his face and head were manicured to perfection. He wore his favorite diamond-encrusted watch and diamond necklace. He looked just as clean as always when seen on the street.

Cookie stayed in the shadows. She didn't want to interact with a bunch of phony people constantly saying, "He looks good," and "If you need anything let me know."

Cookie left before the memorial was over. She could no longer bear the sight of Tiger lying in the casket, and tomorrow would be the final goodbye. She needed some alone time. She had someone take her home; but first, she convinced them to drive her by her and Tiger's old house.

It had been over four years. There was a new family staying inside, but it looked the same. She stared through the window at where she once called home. Where she thought she would raise her family. Now a new family would be living her dream.

As she was thinking of all the great times in the home, she also remembered the day this nightmare started—the day Det. Holzendorf and the JSO force disrupted their peace. She wiped away a tear and had the driver take her home.

* * *

TIGERS FUNERAL

As expected, hundreds of guests showed up to Tiger's funeral. People were standing along the wall, while others hovered around the exit. People were even outside waiting to see Tiger's casket for the last time. The church was set up like a wedding. Baby angel images were hanging from the ceiling. The choir wore white robes with golden sashes across the chest, matching Tiger's suit.

Cookie sat up front with Ms. Kat, Tiger's aunt, Ace's daughter, and her Aunt Steph, who was a member of the church and did most of the decorations.

The pastor spoke words of Tiger the best he could, based on the little he learned. He tried to console the family with scripture based on God's word. "It's apparent based on the turnout here today, that Brother Antonio McMillan was known by many. Some may say even loved by most," the pastor began. "But the real question we need to ask ourselves about Brother McMillan, and about ourselves, ladies and gentlemen, is: are we known by God?"The crowd moaned in agreement as the pastor continued.

"We can have a million Facebook friends, and a million TikTok subscribers, but none of that matters when God opens the Lamb Book of Life and your name isn't in it."

He grabbed the mic and walked to the front of the pulpit.

"How many likes you get, and how many views you got won't help you when God shows you the view of the life you lived from His view. So, I say to you all today: REPENT!"

Cookie looked up with calming eyes, listening to the pastor as he ended with, "'Cause the last thing you ever wanna hear is God say the words: depart from me; I never knew you."

The crowd cheered as the pastor turned Tiger's homegoing into a church service.

When the pastor was done speaking, he asked the family if they wanted to say a few words on behalf of the dearly departed.

The pastor stared at Cookie, but she couldn't move. She was too distraught to speak at the time. When it seemed no family would come up to speak, Tiger's cousin Warren—who Tiger didn't speak with much anymore because he was on drugs—decided to come up.

Warren didn't have much money, so he wasn't properly dressed for a funeral, or anywhere for that matter. But Tiger was his family, and no one would stop him from attending.

"Good evening, everyone," Warren began.

"I'm Warren, Antonio's screw-up of a cousin." Small laughs came from the crowd, as people wondered who this homeless-looking guy was. "Y'all knew my cuz as Tiger; but growing up we called him Tsilm T."

Cookie listened on as Warren told stories of Tiger that she never knew but was amazed by. The crowd laughed hysterically when Warren told a story of when they were playing high school football. Tiger felt it would be funny to scratch his butt crack, then convince the coach to smell it by telling the coach he grabbed something from his office and he couldn't identify the smell. Cookie felt Warren, despite his dress appearance, did a phenomenal job enlightening the crowd of who Antonio, Tiger, or Tilsm T really was.

She felt she did have something to say now. There was another part of Tiger they needed to know also—the loving, nurturing boyfriend. As she was about to begin, looking out into the crowd from the pulpit, she caught eyes with who she considered to be the devil himself: Detective Mark Anthony Holzendorf.

He was escorted by two uniformed officers. He nodded at Cookie, then turned and walked outside. He wanted her to know he was there for her, but he would allow her this moment.

Cookie gave a heart-warming rendition of her life with Tiger. During the funeral, the crowd cried, praised, laughed, and cried some more. The love was genuine. People who haven't seen each other in years reunited once again.

After the service was done, and Tiger was placed at his final resting place, Cookie walked over to Holzendorf to bring this to an end.

"Sorry about ya loss," the Detective began. Cookie didn't acknowledge his words with a response.

"If it's any consolation, I didn't want it to end like this. He drew his gun, and I had no choice."*HE WAS ON THE GROUND, BITCH!* Cookie wanted to say.

"What do you want?" Cookie asked with an attitude.

"We gotta bring you in for questioning."

"About?" Cookie cut in quickly.

"Your name came up in the involvement of a couple unsolved murders. We would like to get your side of what's going on."

"Sure," Cookie stated, wanting to stab Holzendorf in the chest.

"Let me make a call really quick."

Cookie dialed up her lawyer and told him she was being taken in for questioning and to meet her downtown.

* * *

Inside the interrogation room, Cookie was briefed on the accusations brought against her. "Thanks for coming out today," Det. Holzendorf began.

"I am Det. Mark Holzendorf, and this is Det. Mike Smith from the homicide division."

"How can we assist you gentlemen this fine evening?" Cookie's lawyer asked calmly.

"We'll cut straight to the chase." He turned his attention toward Cookie.

"Do you know a Josh Williamson?"

Cookie nodded no, not giving much thought to the question.

"What about a Rashod Williams, known to the streets as Tank?"

Cookie thought for a moment as the Detective pulled out pictures of both of the men in question.

She looked at the pictures as Holzendorf added, "Both of these guys are dead; and coincidentally, your name came up in the involvement of their death."

"Is there a question here?" Cookie's lawyer asked, then added, "Or the better question is, is there any evidence other than circumstantial hearsay?"

Neither detective had any hard evidence; and their prime witness was one of the deceased. Cookie's lawyer disproved and debunked any accusation the detectives threw at her. Cookie didn't have to say much, being the lawyer requested they present any evidence they had and the cause for such questioning.

She enjoyed watching Det. Holzendorf and his colleague crash and burn against her lawyer. He was expensive, but worth every penny.

"Well," Cookie's lawyer stated calmly as he stood up. "I feel we've been more than cooperative with you gentlemen. So if we're done here, or no charges are being brought against my client, we will bid you guys adieu."

Cookie slowly got up, constantly keeping intense contact with Detective Holzendorf. She gave him an evil grin. He knew at that moment that she played him. She sashayed past Holzendorf like she was untouchable.

"Have a good one, gentlemen," she stated sarcastically as she walked through the door her lawyer was holding open for her.

Before she completely exited, she turned and stated, "Good luck, guys."

Cookie walked out the interrogation building feeling delightful. She took a deep breath. The air seemed to smell much fresher for some strange reason, and the sky was a more radiant shade of blue.

As she started to step off the curb to head across the street where her car was parked, she felt a little woozy. She paused for a moment to gather her composure. What was that? she thought to herself, taking a deep breath. Was she hungry? Was she dehydrated?

There was a water with lemon in the cup holder in her car; she just had to get there. "That's some lawyer ya got there," Holzendorf stated when he saw Cookie still outside as he came out to smoke a cigarette.

"I know he set you back a pretty penny. Wonder how you're able to afford him?"

Cookie chose not to respond. She was starting to see spots but didn't wanna ask Holzendorf for help; he may take her to jail instead of the hospital.

Cookie turned and attempted to step toward her car again as Holzendorf added,

"I know you had something to do with these murders somehow. And with ya boyfriend dead, and you still able to afford a lawyer like him, it tells me he left you a lil drug money somewhere."

Cookie took two steps toward her car, turned toward Holzendorf, then collapsed in the middle of the crosswalk.

* * *

Heavy had been in custody for over six weeks. He was denied bond, being he had access to an unknown amount of funds. The state labeled him a flight risk.

They were using all their resources to build a concrete case on Heavy. He made the bold call to not waive his rights for a speedy trial. He challenged the prosecutors to build a case with minimal time and the evidence they had thus far.

He was facing up to 60 years if found guilty; according to the prosecutors the first time they talked with him. He felt if they were gonna go for an outlandish sentence, he wouldn't give them maximum time to railroad him.

"The state is getting nervous," Heavy's lawyer stated happily. "They now offering 15 to life; I turned it down."

"Damn right, turn that down," Heavy stated confidently.

"If they got something, tell them to bring it." There was a slight pause, and the lawyer stated, "I have some other news. Good or bad depending on how you look at it."

"Here we go. Here comes the bull shit," Heavy responded in wonder.

Heavy's lawyer pulled out a picture and asked, "Do you know this young lady?"

Heavy glanced at the picture and nodded.

"Yeah, that's my homeboy girl; that's Cookie.""Some detectives been talking with her a lot. Questioning her about some murders she may or may not been involved in."

"Nah, man. She a good girl," Heavy confirmed calmly.

"Well, it's been brought to my attention that the state plans to subpoena her in your case as a witness."

"WITNESS! For what?" Heavy spat.

"Apparently, she was at your club the night the DEA came up in there, but they let her go for some reason."

Heavy thought back to that night. Cookie was indeed there. But she would never take the stand for the state. She a ride-or-die type of chic, he thought.

"Cookie won't turn state," Heavy stated, convinced. "She solid people."

"You sure?" the lawyer asked again.

"I'm super positive," Heavy snapped.

"Okay." His lawyer spoke unconvinced, as he added, "Be aware, I'm sure they gonna scare her with an indictment on those murders if she refuses to take the stand, testifying that those drugs were yours."

Heavy thought for a moment. Cookie took the charge for Tiger, but what would be her motivation to risk her freedom for his? He had some thinking to do. Or should he cut his losses and take those 15 years.

13

The Queen's Move

Cookie woke up in the hospital. She had been unconscious for 2 days. She slowly looked around at her surroundings. She didn't remember how she got there, nor anything after leaving the interrogation office. There was an IV in her arm, administering fluids into her body, and a pulse-ox on her finger to monitor her oxygen levels.

Channel 9 News was broadcasting the weather, and Cookie noticed the date was 2 days later than she remembered. Cookie felt well rested, but her body was still a little weak. She could hear commotion in the hallway, a mixture of footsteps, voices, and beeping monitors from other rooms.

Her mouth was dry, and she was hungry. The liquid food they were pumping through her blood wasn't cutting it; she craved seafood.

She was about to call the nurses station when she noticed her lawyer enter her room.

"Knock, knock," he spoke, tapping on the door hinge.

"Heeey, Dorsey," she began, reaching for the nurse button.

"What are you doing here?"

"I received a call after I left, saying you collapsed in the street and were rushed here to Baptist."

He walked closer and placed a flowerpot with a cactus inside on the table.

"Really, Phil," she laughed. "A cactus?"

"Flowers die after a few days. A cactus lasts for years."

Cookie laughed, then stated, "I wish you woulda brought me something to eat. A bitch hungry."

"I have something better for you, right here." Dorsey handed Cookie a piece of paper as he read the contents from the copy he held.

"What is this?" Cookie wondered.

"This is Antonio McMillan's last will and testament documents. Along with a copy of his life insurance policy he took on himself in case of his death."

She glanced over the paperwork, noticing large amounts on each document, and her name in the beneficiary area. Her heart rate elevated, causing a spike in her heart monitor as Dorsey continued.

"I need your signature here," Dorsey began, handing Cookie a pen. "When everything clears through probate court, you will be the new possessor of the late Antonio McMillan estate."Consisting of an 8,000 sq. ft. home in Marsh Landing. Also, he had stocks in Bitcoin, J.P. Morgan, and Shib totaling 425 thousand in investments. And lastly—" he spoke as Cookie began crying happy tears.

She was broke and would have had nothing after today.

"There is a term-life insurance policy he had on himself naming you the beneficiary in the amount of—"

He paused for a moment as Cookie anticipated the amount.

"One! Million! Dollars!"

Cookie took several deep breaths to calm her heart rate. Her constant spike on her heart monitor caught the attention of the on-duty nurse.

"What's going on in here?" she asked, pushing numbers on Cookie's heart rate machine.

"Nothing!" Cookie stated with happy tears on her face.

"Everything's absolutely perfect."

The nurse wasn't convinced. If her rate continued, she may have a cardiac arrest.

"Well, I'ma be going," Lawyer Dorsey stated, gathering his paperwork. "I gotta get this paperwork updated and faxed by this evening."

"Yes. You do that," Cookie added, then laid back in her bed.

The nurse watched as Cookie's heart rate slowed down to normal within seconds.

"With your condition, you can't be getting that excited, ma'am," the nurse commented.

"With my condition?" Cookie asked, sitting up. "Why am I here?"

"The doctor will be in shortly to brief you on any questions you may have about your condition."

Cookie laid back once again, closing her eyes, relaxing, and thanking God for turning around her situation.

"Hellooooo," a voice stated, followed by a couple light knocks on her room door.

Cookie slowly opened her eyes to see Big Lez walking through the door.

"I know you fucking lying," Cookie snapped as Lez slowly walked in carrying yellow roses.

"NUUUUURSE!" Cookie yelled, looking for the nurse's station button.

Lez tried to calm Cookie down. Cookie was angrily distraught. Lez pleaded just for a moment of her time to explain.

"I DON'T HAVE SHIT TO SAY TO YOU!" Cookie blurted loudly.

"Okay," Lez spoke humbly. "Then let me talk." "What makes you think I wanna hear anything you gotta say!" Cookie spoke through gritted teeth.

"Pleeeeease," Lez asked.

Cookie got quiet, laid her head back, and turned her head away from Lez. Lez noticed Cookie was breathing heavily, but she wasn't demanding her to leave, so Lez took that as her opportunity to explain her side to the best of her ability.

"First off, I would like to say I am soooo sorry. Me and Tiger's situation is waaaay more complicated than it seems."

"Complicated!" Cookie chimed in, trying to keep her composure.

"Weren't y'all fucking?"

Lez dropped her head, ashamed, as Cookie continued. "You may as well be honest now. The shit's out in the open. Weren't y'all fucking?"

Lez nodded, wiping away a tear.

"And when you pregnant, the babies were his, right?"

Lez once again nodded.

"Don't seem complicated to me," Cookie snapped, turning her head again. "Seems cut and fucking dry."

Lez hadn't prepared for Cookie to speak. She was hoping to clear her conscience and then leave. But this was a situation that had to be faced now rather than later if they were gonna get past this.

"Yes. Tiger and I have slept together on a few occasions," Lez began, then continued.

"But it wasn't on some random sneaky link type shit. I loved him."

Cookie looked to face Lez after she made the comment.

"I did. I loved him. Very much."

Cookie could see in her eyes she was actually in love. It takes a strong woman to tell another woman in her face that she loves her man—and still wants to be her friend.

"It wasn't my plan to love Tiger, let alone even like him. I was 19 when I first came to Jacksonville. I had almost nothing. I got off the Greyhound with the clothes on my back, 65 dollars, and a Walmart bag with two outfits in it that my cousin gave me when I left Carolina. I had no family here, so I did what most young girls in my situation would do; I started stripping. I was terrible at it, but most older guys didn't care. If you got tits and ass and you cute, you can make money. The money wasn't always great, but I kept a hotel room, and I ate—fast food mostly."

"I needed to fit in, so I entered into a domestic relationship with a guy named J.B.

"J.B. was a particular type of dude. He was a short, stocky fella who was known around Duval as a jack-boy. But he only robs dope boys, and not just any dope boys; the crem de la crem.

"One evening Tiger, Pieyay, and Heavy came into Cocktails, and the girls in the club got lit. I didn't know who they were at the time, but just from the look of the group, I could tell Tiger was a boss. Everyone else was flashy, loud, wanted to be seen, but Tiger sat back. I mean, he tipped a little and drunk his drank; but he lingered in the shadows.

"J.B., though, knew exactly who he was, and he wanted me to seduce him and lure him into an ambush to be robbed. And at first, I tried. I asked Tiger did he want a dance, he turned me down. I touched him, and he politely eased me away. So I asked did he have a girlfriend, and he quickly said yes.'

Cookie tried to hide her smile, not wanting Lez to think she was even listening to her story, as Lez continued.

"So I walked over to J.B. and told him this guy was a no-go. I mean, Tiger wouldn't give me no play at all. Girl, J.B. grabbed me by my neck and told me if I don't make that happen, he was gonna beat my ass, kill me, then throw me into Trout River.

"I was petrified of that man."

"I guess Tiger must have assumed J.B. was my pimp or something, 'cause we caught eyes when I was being choked, and he turned his eyes away, then occasionally looked back to see if I was okay."

"When I walked back over near Tiger and Heavy, Tiger pulled me to the side and gave me a hunnit dollars. I guess he felt I didn't make enough to satisfy J.B.

"I looked in his eyes and knew he was different. He cared about people—a dangerous trait in this game—but he did.

"I threw all caution to the wind at that moment. I told Tiger about J.B.'s plan to rob him or worse, and if I don't deliver, he was gonna kill me."

The nurse came in to check on Cookie. She set a lunch tray alongside her bed for her to eat when ready. Lez nodded with a fake grin, waited 'til the nurse left, then continued.

Cookie was hungry, but she wanted to hear the rest of the story uninterrupted.

"Where was I?" Lez thought. "Oh yeah. I told Tiger his plan, and he told me to set it up as planned; and he'll handle the rest.

"When J.B. got to the meeting spot, thinking he had the upper hand, Tiger ambushed him instead.

"They beat J.B. almost to death. It was a beautiful sight." Lez smiled, then continued.

"I was given a choice by Tiger to either leave Jacksonville and never return—because shit was gonna get sticky—or I could prove I was a ride-or-die chic and put in some work.

"I chose to be a rider; and he told me I had to shoot and kill J.B. right there.

"I shot my crappy-ass boyfriend without a second thought."

Lez placed the flowers she had for Cookie on the desk. Cookie hadn't budged, so Lez finished. "The next few months, Tiger kept me welded to his hip. He gave me the game. How to cook dope, measure coke, how to aim and shoot a gun, how to count money, and he got me that apt in Ken Knight. He transformed Leslie Hill into Big Lez." "I owed him and vowed that I would be forever loyal to him and his team. He is a brilliant man.""So that's when y'all started fucking?" Cookie spat with an attitude.

"No!" Lez snapped back. "Can I finish, please?"Cookie let out a heavy sigh, then continued listening.

"We were like Bonnie and Clyde, and I was gaining street cred from living off his coattail. He would be with me from early morning to late nights. But he would always let me know he had to get home to his girl—you.

"You were his everything. I had never met you, but I almost knew everything about you. I even helped pick out that bracelet he got you for y'all fourth anniversary."

Cookie remembered that bracelet. That was actually her favorite piece of jewelry.

"I must admit," Lez rerouted back. "I was jealous of you and Tiger's unwavering bond."

Lez walked over, placed her hands on Cookie's, but Cookie quickly removed her hand. Lez was hurt, realizing the damage she caused to a true friend. She continued with the story, hoping to cleanse her spirit and break free of this torment she had been living with ever since she solidified her bond with Cookie.

"Over the years, I began to see Tiger with different eyes. A respect turned to like, like turned to a crush, crush turned to a lust, and eventually I started having thoughts—real naughty thoughts."

Cookie didn't wanna hear this shit. This was actually the moment she felt she should be whooping Lez ass.

"The sexual boundary between me and Tiger was crossed January 19th, on my birthday almost five years ago.

"A group of us were hanging out. Tiger had gotten a little tipsy, and as you know, he wasn't much of a drinker. I didn't think he should drive, so I had one of the chics from the club take us both home, 'cause I was a bit wasted myself.

"We dropped Tiger off first, then me, and I let my girl take my car home, and she was supposed to bring it back in the morning.

"About an hour after I had showered and laid down, I was struggling trying to sleep because I was kinda sexually frustrated. I grabbed my trusted rose friend and was about to get it in, when I heard constant loud banging on my door. I was livid. I tried to ignore it, but they were determined. I stormed to the door pissed, pistol in hand.

"I opened the door angry, tired, eyes blurry and horny as hell. And standing at my door, as if he was a gift from Satan himself, was Tiger. He said you had made him leave. He say you said something about who was some girl he just brought to y'all house. I don't honestly remember; I was tipsy and Tiger was at my house."

Cookie remembered that day. She'd been calling Tiger's phone for hours with no response. She heard a car pull up in her yard, she looked out the window and saw Tiger get out a car with two women inside. When asked where his car was, he couldn't remember, and he claimed he didn't know the girl who dropped him off. She told him to go back to the bitch who brought him home and refused to let him sleep unless he left.

"We were both tired and tipsy," Lez continued. "But I was also sexually aroused. Tiger apparently thought he was home, 'cause he stripped down to his boxers and collapsed on my bed. I watched for a moment, taking it all in." "He was sleeping comfortably, but I definitely couldn't sleep at this point. I did as he did, I got undressed, climbed in bed with him. And———"

Before she could finish, Cookie turned to face her, giving her an evil eye. Lez realized that would be the stopping point of that story, but Cookie edged it on.

"And what?" Cookie spat out.

Lez stayed quiet.

"And that's when you fucked my man."

In Lez head, that's what happened, but Cookie made it sound so horrible and evil. Technically, you sent your man to me, Lez thought.

"We…" Lez paused for a moment, struggling to get out the words. "We… we slept together, yes." "Unprotected!" Cookie cut in quickly.

Maybe this wasn't the best idea, Lez thought.

Cookie was making her confession and attempt to regain her friendship seem like Lez was a shepherd for the devil.

"Sis. I am soooo sorry," Lez pleaded. "The time when these events took place, I didn't know you. And I know that don't make it right," Lez quickly added, noticing Cookie turning, about to snap at that comment.

"I was young. I was lonely. I was playing a man's game, and I had a front-row seat to what a real king may have looked like in medieval times. He was a boss in every sense of the word, and I fell deeply in love with him over time.

"And this may sound harsh, but him having a girlfriend wasn't my concern back then. My whole reason of being became to prove to this man I was her. But regardless of what we ever done, you were his everything. And I eventually came to terms with that.

"The love never wavered, but my approach did. And when I got to actually meet you, I see why he love you so much. You are a beautiful soul." "Did he tell you to come get me from jail?" Cookie asked, feeling a bit more understanding to Lez's situation.

She was still pissed Lez ever slept with her man, but she understood Lez's reasoning behind it. Tiger was a great person to all.

"Yes," Lez nodded. "He always wanted me to meet you, and he felt that would be a better time than any."

Cookie finally cracked a slight smile as she asked, "And what about that night in your shower? What was that about?"

"Oh, that was just me, girl," Lez joked. "You fine as shit."

Cookie thought back to that evening. It was a vulnerable moment in her life.

"Prison do strange thangs to a woman," Cookie joked, as Lez smiled, happy that Cookie was talking to her again.

"Speaking of prison," Lez cut back in. "I took care of that Felicia problem for ya."

"Oh really!" Cookie asked with a devilish smirk. "Do tell."

"As fate would have it, I know a C.O. in there named Derek. He used to always try to holla at me back in the day."

"I know Derek," Cookie spat. "He try to talk to everybody."

"Yeah, he told me he remembered you. And that you were a character."

Cookie smiled thinking back. She missed Keli, but outside of that, jail was horrible.

"I promised I would let him taste the rainbow if he handled something for me. He was hooked, line and sinker at that point.

"I had him take me through there and introduce me to a 'bout-it bitch who wanted to put in some work for some commissary. Several bitches were willing to off this chic for a peanut butter squeeze and an iced honey bun.

"I told Derek I wanted to see it on tape to verify the deed was done, so here it is."

Lez pulled out her phone, selected the video Derek sent to her from his phone gallery. She walked over to Cookie, and they watched the video. The video showed Felicia and Sasha being ambushed by five inmates with shanks in the shower.

Cookie laughed as Felicia and Sasha screamed like pigs for the guards, as the girls—two of which Cookie knew—were stabbing Felicia and Sasha severely. By the time the other officers rushed to help, you could hear Derek rushing in as if concerned, and the tape ended.

Cookie was satisfied; Keli would have been also.

"And that only cost me a carton of cigarettes and two boxes of iced honey buns."

"And some Skittles," Cookie joked in.

"I ain't buy nobody any Skittles."

"Well, you say you gonna let Derek taste the rainbow."

They both laughed, then Lez continued.

"I'm heading back to North Carolina this week." Lez switched the subject, dampening the mood. Cookie gave a stunned look as Lez added,

"I done got all I was supposed to get out of Jacksonville. This new set of hustlers got the game all twisted. They kill, steal, and snitch; nobody grinds anymore. I felt I should cut my losses before someone come for me for all the bullshit I did in my life."

She paused for a moment as Cookie and her caught eyes.

"I'ma truly miss you, my sister," Lez commented, leaning in for a hug from Cookie, and she embraced her back.

"Come with me!" Lez spoke excitedly.

Cookie pondered Lez's invitation to relocate. She had no real ties to Jacksonville anymore being Tiger was dead. Her Aunt Steph and Ms. Kat, Tiger's aunt, were all she had left. She also felt that as long as she was seen in Jacksonville, Detective Holzendorf would never leave her alone. Maybe out of sight, out of mind may work in her favor.

As she was about to respond to Lez about going with her to Carolina, the doctor walked in, glancing down at a folder.

"Ms. Loveless," he spoke, walking up to her bed and clasping her hand into his.

"Glad to see you're up. You gave us quite a scare a few days ago."

"What's going on, Doc? How did I end up here?""Well, when you came in, we couldn't ask you any questions because you were unconscious.""We noticed you had severe hemorrhaging in the vaginal region. We did an ultrasound and we discovered that you have polysymptomatic ovarian cysts on your uterus.

"To prevent the need for a blood transfusion, we need to immediately prep you for surgery if there will be any chance to save your baby. We think time is of the essence."

The doctor tried to continue explaining Cookie's condition, but she was stumped on a statement he quickly brushed over as if the words never came out of his mouth.

"Doc, excuse me," she mumbled, but he continued trying to push forward.

"DOC!" Cookie spoke louder, gaining his attention.

"Go back a few sentences. Preferably around the part where you was explaining why it's important that we rush this surgery."

The doctor looked at Cookie confused, but he also noticed her confused look and stated, "Oh... you didn't know."

"Know what, Doc?" Cookie and Lez paused, waiting for his repeated "Congratulations. You're pregnant."

The End

www.ingramcontent.com/pod-product-compliance
Lightning Source LLC
Chambersburg PA
CBHW060649260626
47161CB00008B/3068